INFORMED CONSENT

Recent Titles by Peter Turnbull from Severn House

The Hennessey and Yellich Series

AFTER THE FLOOD
ALL ROADS LEADETH
CHELSEA SMILE
CHILL FACTOR
THE DANCE MASTER
DARK SECRETS
DEATHTRAP
FALSE KNIGHT
FIRE BURN
INFORMED CONSENT
NO STONE UNTURNED
ONCE A BIKER
PERILS AND DANGERS
THE RETURN
TREASURE TROVE
TURNING POINT

SWEET HUMPHREY

INFORMED CONSENT

A Hennessey and Yellich Mystery

by

Peter Turnbull

severn House

This first world edition published 2009
in Great Britain and in the USA by
SEVERN HOUSE PUBLISHERS LTD of
9–15 High Street, Sutton, Surrey, England, SM1 1DF.
Trade paperback edition published
in Great Britain and the USA 2009 by
SEVERN HOUSE PUBLISHERS LTD

British Library Cataloguing in Publication Data

Turnbull, Peter, 1950-
  Informed consent
  1. Hennessey, George (Fictitious character) - Fiction
  2. Yellich, Somerled (Fictitious character) - Fiction
  3. Police - England - Yorkshire - Fiction 4. Murder -
  Investigation - England - Yorkshire - Fiction 5. Detective
  and mystery stories
  I. Title
    823.9'14 [F]

ISBN-13: 978-0-7278-6751-3   (cased)
ISBN-13: 978-1-84751-124-9   (trade paper)

Typeset by Palimpsest Book Production Ltd.,
Grangemouth, Stirlingshire, Scotland.
Printed and bound in Great Britain by
MPG Books Ltd., Bodmin, Cornwall.

ONE

The body, for that was what it was, only became a body upon closer inspection. Patrick 'Chalkie' White's beat was the centre of the small and ancient city and it was, he had found, and him being a long-serving man, a pleasingly busy beat for a police officer and he considered himself privileged. In these days when old-fashioned foot patrols have been largely, but only largely, replaced by mobile patrols in cars, he felt lucky to have a beat at all, and was doubly lucky that his beat was busy. A busy beat, he found, went rapidly and also left him with the satisfaction of feeling he had done his job; 'earned his crust' as his mother used to say. His beat was particularly hectic up to 22.00 hours during the afternoon shift, and the night shift from 22.00 hours until midnight was similarly frenetic: the drunks to be arrested, the fights to break up, and the car accidents to attend with the other emergency services, often largely due to abuse of alcohol. Patrick White would frequently wonder in moments of private reflection about the hue and cry made about narcotics and other illegal substances, when, should such matter be removed from the United Kingdom, the Accident and Emergency Departments of the hospitals would, he believed, still be just as full with the dying and severely injured, and the corpses in the mortuaries would still be just as plentiful. Most often because of alcohol. After midnight, York, being a city in name only, more of a small town in actuality, calmed and quietened and seemed to become his and almost his alone, sharing it only with the occasional all-night bus, and the equally occasional taxi. The mobile patrols in the area cars would flash their headlights in greeting as they slowly passed and he, in turn, would respond with a raised hand or a flash of his torch. His was the policing of the older style. In the twenty-first century, when policing was done by mobile patrols and CCTV, there was in Patrick White's opinion, nothing to 'beat the bobby on the beat', or as was often also said, 'can't beat a beat bobby'. It was a view shared by the public, who would give welcoming smiles of approval when he encountered them. By 02.00 hours the city had become as fully calm and as silent as Patrick White believed it was going to be. Nonetheless, he still found work to do. His very presence, the echoing measured tread of his boots, reassured anyone still awake and that, he believed, was work in itself. He would check doors of business premises, ensuring that they were locked, and finding other similar work to do as he relished the poignancy that settles over the city at night.

He had been a police officer for a long time and he still loved the sense of 'touching' a city, 'touching' his beat which he could never seem to achieve in the few months he spent as a mobile patrol officer, or when he sat for hours on end in front of a CCTV monitor screen. He had had a word with his watch leader, just a polite and a relaxed chat, and shortly thereafter he was back walking the beat, loving the sense of protecting the ancient and reputedly most haunted city in Britain, but which had never presented himself with a sight or a sound which he could not explain. White tended to walk the thoroughfares of the town, but occasionally would allow himself to venture into a snickel-way, one of the system of alleyways which he felt were like a street system within a street system, particularly the larger snickelways such as Mad Alice Lane and Coffee Yard. But in the main, Patrick White kept to the roads, it was, he believed, where he was most needed and where he was most needed to be seen. He had, like all beat officers, his 'dive(s)', a place where he would be invited in, a mug of tea or coffee pressed into his hand, often spliced with a small measure of whiskey or rum, and as such would be particularly welcome on a cold and damp night. 'Dives' tended to be few and far between in the dead hours of the 'graveyard' shift when the ghostly silence in the 1,000-year-old city was broken only by his footfall and the distant klaxon from a passing train rumbling through the night, south to London, or north to Scotland. There were, however, 'dives' that Patrick White had cultivated over the years, the Fire Station, always open, the hut used by the taxi drivers, the offices of the Transport Police at the railway station, the premises of the out of hours Social Work Department team, all had an ever open door policy, all with a bottomless teapot and, if he was lucky, a toasted sandwich or two.

It was just after one such hospitality stop that night at the Transport Police, that Patrick White, police constable, once again walked calmly into the night, turning left beside the cholera pits, following the walls, as cold and as grey as the Minster, glistening with rain. He turned right by the war memorial and walked beside the black and silent river, along the twentieth-century development of Riverside Walk and, as he did so, noticed that the precipitation was increasing as the relentless and annoying drizzle had turned into rainfall proper. PC White crossed the river at Ouse Bridge and walked up the short incline that was Low Ousegate. All was silent at that point. At the crossroads he turned left beside St Michael's Church and entered Spurriergate and then he saw what appeared to be two black refuse sacks lying in the road, carelessly and selfishly discarded, wantonly 'fly tipped' in the street and left for someone else to dispose of. He had not noticed them when he had walked the street just an hour or two earlier, they had therefore been dumped very, very recently. As White approached the bags trying to focus his eyes in the gloom, pierced only by dim street lamps and a full moon, they began to appear to be less and less like two refuse bags lying close together, and became more like a single large bag, and then the mound, lying in the gutter came to be seen for what it was; a human being.

The person, so far as the spill of Patrick White's torch beam and the artificial light from street lamps and shop front windows allowed him to discern, was an adult male. Middle-aged, White thought, reasonably well dressed it seemed, and so far as he could tell, when he felt the man's pulse points, his neck and wrists, he was dead, quite, quite dead. The body had no heat and was beginning to feel clammy. From White's experience, though he was no qualified medical man, he concluded that he had encountered a corpse. He stood calmly and reached for the radio which was attached to his tunic collar.

Thomson Ventnor approached the body with quiet reverence and knelt and peeled back the black plastic sheet which by then had been placed over the corpse. He too saw what Constable White had earlier seen: a late-middle-aged man, well dressed; the man wore an expensive-looking watch, good quality clothing, he had neatly trimmed silver hair, clean shaven; he had the full face and fleshy hands of a well-nourished person. Ventnor glanced at his watch 02.44 hours. He replaced the sheet and stood and looked at White, questioningly.

'I didn't think that it was a body at first, sir.' White addressed Ventnor, in keeping with his status, despite Ventnor being much the younger man. For White, age was not an issue, rank though, was everything. 'Very dark, poorly lit and the rain didn't help at all, dimmed the street lamps and also what light came from the shop windows.'

'Yes.' Ventnor glanced about him, the dark February sky, the low cloud and the confused light, the doorways, the alley entrances, the shadows. He watched a large rat scurry across Spurriergate, about twenty feet distant, busy about its business, foraging in the damp night, and it seemed, calmly, nonchalantly, unconcerned by the human activity. 'I can see how that could be the case.'

'I thought at first that it was a couple of bin liners full of refuse, lying close together. Thought someone had dumped them in the night, but as I got closer . . . well . . .'

'Yes.' Thomson Ventnor stood again. 'What do you make of it?' He asked with a smile, attempting to lift the mood. '"Iffy", don't you think?'

'Well . . . yes, sir . . .' White struggled with his reply, not responding to Ventnor's smile. The question made him feel complimented as Ventnor's face seemed to flash from light to dark to light as it was caught by the lapping blue lamp of the police vehicle which had conveyed him and two other constables to the scene. 'I mean, I might have thought it a hit-and-run but this street is a pedestrian precinct. Some vehicles come down it though, delivery vehicles, council road cleansing vehicles . . . but "iffy", as you say, sir.'

'Why? Why so "iffy"?' Ventnor continued to smile.

'Well, sir . . . with respect . . . a well-dressed man of his age walking in the city at this hour? I walked this street about two hours earlier, nothing here then but for a man of his age . . . and money . . . not to take a taxi at this hour and in this weather.'

'Yes.' Ventnor nodded. 'But I think you're right, it feels suspicious. I don't think we are dealing with a heart attack.' Ventnor knelt down and peeled the sheet back exposing the head. 'Not really our job to say he is deceased.'

'No, sir.'

Ventnor glanced beyond White as a car slowly approached the scene driving on dipped headlight beams. The car halted behind the police car and a young, slender, turbaned man got out of the car and walked to where Ventnor and White stood. He carried a black Gladstone bag.

'Good morning, sir,' Ventnor said softly as the doctor approached and was in earshot.

'Good morning,' Dr Mann responded with equal softness. 'Where . . .?'

'Just here, sir.' Ventnor and White stepped to one side to allow the police surgeon access to the body.

Dr Mann knelt beside the body and felt for a pulse on the neck and noticeably kept his fingers resting on the artery for considerably longer than either Ventnor or White had done. 'I've got a pulse,' he said with a slightly raised voice. He stood. 'He's alive. The pulse is there . . . just. But it's there.' Patrick White snatched his radio and pressed the send button. 'Ambulance Spurrier Street, please . . . urgent . . . urgent. Middle-aged male, very weak pulse.'

'I'm sorry,' Ventnor stammered, moving to his left and then to his right. 'I felt for a pulse . . . we both did, neither of us found one and he felt deceased . . . very cold to the touch.'

'It's easy to miss,' Dr Mann said, taking off his coat and folding it up to place under the man's head. 'I nearly gave up. And the clamminess, that can be misleading.' Dr Mann put on a pair of latex gloves and felt the man's head, running his fingers over the man's scalp. 'Ah . . .'

'Something, sir?'

'Fractured skull, but no blood, just swelling, very distinct swelling, he seems to have sustained a subdural haematoma, the blood is seeping inwards, going into his brain. It'll have to be drained. I'll phone York District Accident and Emergency, tell them what to expect.' He stood and walked rapidly back to his car, opened the door and reached for his car phone.

'I feel bad about this, sir,' White appealed to Ventnor.

'So do I,' Ventnor replied, his eyes caught by an all-night bus moving slowly down Lower Ousegate at the end of Spurriergate, its driver glancing at the police activity. 'But it was me that covered him with the sheet, not you. That's for me to live with and you did report him as "appears deceased".'

'Yes, sir.'

'Make sure that you put that in your report and also make it clear that you could not detect a pulse and that the skin felt clammy.'

'Yes, sir.'

'Any flak comes about this, then it'll come my way, not yours.'

'Yes, sir. Thank you, sir.'

'But . . . you can't help but feel what you feel, as I can't.'

'No, sir.'

'Well, we can't move him now—' Ventnor looked at the body – 'so you go to the hospital with him. When the medics remove his clothes, you check the pockets. We need his wallet for his ID and anything else that might seem relevant.'

'Yes, sir.'

After the ambulance had arrived, after the injured man had been skilfully placed within and it had departed, after Dr Mann had also departed, his services as police surgeon no longer being required, Ventnor turned to the two remaining constables and said, 'Doubt we'll find anything but we have to search the area.'

'Yes, sir.'

'So, the way he fell indicates that he was walking in that direction—' Ventnor pointed towards Coney Street and the Mansion House – 'as though he came from that direction.' He then pointed towards Lower Ousegate. 'So we'll walk down there. Don't know what we're looking for but we'll look for it anyway.'

'Understood, sir,' said one of the constables.

The three officers walked line abreast to the end of Spurriergate, where upon Ventnor's instruction they split up, with one officer walking up Higher Ousegate, the other walking down Lower Ousegate, and Ventnor walking down short Nessgate and into the longer Castlegate, as far as Tower Street. Thirty minutes later they rendezvoused at the scene of the crime, where the police vehicle stood, still with flashing blue lights. Nothing of suspicion had been noticed or found.

'Had to be done,' Ventnor explained, 'for form's sake. If you could take me to the hospital, please?'

Constable White stood beside the grey metal table in the small anteroom off the Accident and Emergency Department of York City Hospital. The room was about ten feet square, he guessed, painted a uniform shade of cream, smelled strongly of disinfectant, and with the table in the centre of the room, there was little space for a person to move. Ventnor entered the room and he and White held uncomfortable eye contact with both wearing expressions of solemnity. The hospital being in silence at the moment added, it seemed to both men, to the awkward profundity of the moment.

'Anything?' Ventnor asked softly.

'Sir?'

'Well, any news of the victim or anything in the clothing?' He nodded to the pile of clothing atop the polished surface of the table.

'Oh, no news, sir, and I suppose that means "no news is good news" as they say. They are still operating. I haven't looked at the clothing; I was in need of a witness. I like to do things by the book; I am too close to collecting my pension.'

'Yes . . . so, let's look . . . jacket first, seems to be the obvious place to look for a wallet.' Ventnor picked up the jacket reverently by the collar and felt in the inside pocket and extracted a wallet of light-coloured elaborately tooled leather.

'Ah . . .' White commented upon seeing the wallet.

'Significant?' Ventnor asked, still speaking softly.

'Not significant, sir, probably not at least, I just recognize it. Well, I recognize the type I mean.'

'Really?'

'Yes, sir. My daughter and son-in-law bought one like that back from Sardinia. They went on holiday there one year and they brought half a dozen back with them and gave them to friends and relatives, nothing special, just as sold to the tourists. It's that very light-coloured leather and the tooling I recognize, it's pretty well identical to the one I have. Only use it for special occasions, you don't get wallets like that sold in England.'

'Don't, do you.' Ventnor turned the wallet over in his hands, it was larger than most wallets, he thought, about, he estimated, the size of a modest paperback book. It was also very bulky.

'About twice the size of a UK wallet,' White observed. 'Pity I never had twice the amount of money to put in it.'

Ventnor smiled. He much appreciated the humour. He felt it was sorely needed. 'Indeed, same here, we don't get paid much but we see life.' He opened the wallet which was clasped by a press-stud of tortoiseshell, and read the identification within. 'He is one Edwin Hoole, of Workhouse Lane, East Cowton.' Ventnor glanced at White. 'East Cowton?'

'Village near Malton, sir. Monied area.'

'Why doesn't that surprise me?' He opened the fold of the wallet. 'My . . . not short of a bob or two, was he?'

'Seems not, sir.' White glanced at the wad of notes in the wallet.

'Significant though.' Ventnor pressed the wallet shut with a click of the stud. 'We can rule out robbery as a motive for the attack.' He placed the wallet in a manilla envelope beside the pile of clothes. Ventnor glanced at the clothing, all seemed to him to be of high quality. 'Shoes?'

'Oh, under the table, sir, seemed unlucky to put them on the table. I thought the gentleman, Mr Hoole, needed all the luck he can get.'

'Indeed.' Ventnor paused. 'I'd better go and break some bad news. It's bad enough breaking news like this to anyone, but banging on their front door at this hour in order to do it . . .'

'Yes, sir. Do you need assistance?'

'No . . . no, thanks . . . if you could radio for someone to represent the police at the hospital, then return to your beat.'

'Yes, sir.'

'Well, at least the gentleman is still alive, I could be banging on the door with worse news, it still could be worse if he has sustained a subdural haematoma . . . that is potentially fatal.'

'Really? I haven't heard of that.'

'It's just one of those things you pick up.' Ventnor buttoned up his overcoat. 'It's one of the things you remember but, when I was in uniform, I attended a report of a drunk in a park in the city I worked in then. Me and another constable followed up a complaint from a member of the public and just as reported, we found a young man . . . well, fella in his thirties, but young enough, slumped on a park bench, trousers down round his ankles, dried vomit down his front, totally out for the count, gang of children around him just gawping or shouting at him, as kids do. We growled at them and they ran off. We tried to wake him . . . we couldn't find a pulse as you and I couldn't with Mr Hoole, but in that case there really was no pulse to be had.'

'Vomited and suffocated on the stuff, sir?' White suggested. 'I have come across that cause of death often.'

'No—' Ventnor shook his head – 'sadly, no. At the hospital it was discovered that he had suffered massive head injuries.'

'Oh . . . a victim?'

'Yes, but it's a bit worse than that. We made enquiries and we found a string of witnesses and evidence of a fight close to where he was found. He was set on in the early evening, in the summer time of the year. He was probably . . . or was probably taken for, a gay boy . . . such happens.'

'Yes, sir.'

'Anyway, we pieced together what happened or what seemed likely to have happened. We think that he picked himself up and staggered to hospital, knowing he needed help. He got to the A and E Department, hardly able to stand, slurring his speech, holding his trousers up with one hand, reaching forward with the other and the guy at the reception desk with his tie tied into a little knot, and his hair slicked down, so proud of his starched white coat without any medical training whatsoever turned him away because he was drunk. The poor bloke was so out of it and in such a state of shock that he didn't protest, didn't fight his corner, he just turned round, meek and biddable as you please, and walked out as if on autopilot right back to the place he'd been attacked, as if it was the only place he could think of to go once the hospital staff had rejected him . . . and when he got back there, back to the park, back to the very place in the park that he had been attacked, he sat down and died. But he had suffered a subdural haematoma. That's what it does, the head injury caused the blood to seep inwardly and somehow, when it came into contact with his brain it induced symptoms which caused him to appear leglessly drunk. That poor guy hadn't a fluid ounce of alcohol in his system. Anyway, that's the first time I came across the injury. So Dr Mann's diagnosis rang bells. So if something similar happened here, in this case, there's no telling where he was attacked or how far he had walked before collapsing. The fella I told you about, he walked a mile or so to the hospital, and a mile back . . . so you can still cover quite a distance despite the injury. We never got a result for that case; those thugs would probably have been picked up for some other crime. People who do that don't stay without a record, but they got away with that murder anyway as I said, Mr Hoole could have walked for hours either trying to get to the hospital here, or maybe just wandering aimlessly in a semi-comatose state.'

'Due south, sir?'

'I'm sorry?' Ventnor raised his eyebrows. 'Due south, you say?'

'Yes, sir. Well, it's just a thought, sir. If he was wandering aimlessly as you suggest, I am sure I would have noticed him. I did have a break with the Transport Police but even so, I am sure I would have seen him staggering about but if he came from the south and was trying to get here, then he was taking the most direct route. If he had continued on his route, he would have reached the hospital and that would mean he was taking a northerly direction. He was walking north so he was coming from the south. So the area, the place where he was set upon would be south of Spurriergate. Just a thought, sir,' White repeated.

'And a good one. CCTV will have picked him up once he was in the built-up area but there's no CCTV coverage south of there. I'll make sure Mr Hennessey is aware of your idea.'

'Thank you, sir.'

'Well . . . we know what we are doing. I have to drive out to Cowton . . . East Cowton . . . or whatever.'

'You're mad, totally mad.' The youth shook with rage, fear, anger. 'Off your head . . . total nutter . . .'

The man looked at the youth with an icy gleam in his eyes. He didn't respond.

'We were only told to warn him.'

'We did.' The man spoke coldly, calmly. 'I did some debt collecting work once, and that, back there, that was just a warning . . . just a warning.'

'What's the point of killing someone if you want to warn him?' The youth glanced up at the moon as it was exposed by a gap in the clouds. 'You're mad.'

'He's not dead. Believe me . . . he'll get up; this rain will wake him up. He'll have a sore head, then he'll get the message, then he'll stop asking questions . . . and we'll get paid.'

'Stop the car,' the youth pleaded. 'Just stop the car . . . I need to walk . . . I want to walk.'

'No,' the man spoke firmly, 'I don't want you wandering about ready to blab your mouth to the first filth you see, to the first copper that crosses your path. I'm taking you back to mine. You're walking only when you've calmed down. I'll tell you again later . . . but I'll tell you now, if I think there's any danger of you squealing, any risk, you hit the deck at ninety miles an hour and you . . . you don't get up. Understand? Understand?'

'Yes . . .' the youth stammered with a shaking voice. 'Yes . . . I understand. I won't talk . . . not to no one.'

'Good, because I've been inside. I'm not going back. No way am I going back inside.' He halted the car at a red light. 'No way. No way. No way at all.'

Brooding.

The house had a brooding quality about it. It was the only word Ventnor could think of to describe it.

Brooding.

It was, he thought, a building which despite the silence, despite the hour, just did not seem to be at peace with itself, nor was it seemingly a building at slumber, but it seemed to be moodily pondering upon an issue, upon some perceived slight. It was in complete darkness, not a single light was even dimly burning. That Ventnor expected, though he felt, even out here in the country, a security light would have been a sensible thing to leave switched on.

The house stood in a generous parcel of land, so far as Ventnor could make out in the gloom, and that, given the address and the quality of Edwin Hoole's clothing and wristwatch did not surprise him. What did take Ventnor by surprise was the shape of the building. The house was largely single storey, yet clearly Victorian, wide and squat with a tower of three storeys in a central position, with the wings of the house extending at either side of it and so looking, he thought, like a predator which was poised to leap. The front lawn was wide and expansive; with deep shrubbery at either side and the building itself seemed to nestle into the trees which stood behind it and where upper branches were clearly visible above the roofline of the house. Brooding.

After halting at the open gateway for a few seconds as he absorbed the appearance of the house on the deceptively titled 'Workhouse Lane', and noting the name of the house, for a house of this nature was deserving of a name, to be 'Mirfield', Ventnor drove slowly up the concrete driveway with his headlights on full beam, feeling it to be diplomatic and necessary to herald his arrival, rather than stealthily approach in thief-like silence. Few people he knew, appreciated being taken unawares, and that is particularly so in the rural areas where folk are used to greater personal space than those who live and work in the urban areas. He did though baulk at pumping his car horn. That, he felt, would be too insensitive, too alarming, but a loud car engine and strong headlight beams sweeping across deserted rooms would be appropriate, and indeed it did prove to have the desired effect because, as he approached, a light in a room to the left of the main door was switched on. Ventnor halted the car close to the door and switched off the car headlights, just as a light, as if by automatic compensation, shone from the hallway and a slender figure in a blue dressing gown, accompanied by two barking Dobermans stood just beyond the frosted glass set within the door. Ventnor remained standing by his car but didn't approach the door and watched as the figure within the house reached for the lock to open the door. As the door opened the barking of the dogs was replaced by a deep and a menacing growling.

'Oh . . .' The figure was female, the voice alarmed. The door remained held by a security chain which prevented the dogs from attacking Ventnor, or equally, prevented him forcing his way into the house. 'Who is it? Where is Edwin?'

'Police, ma'am.' Ventnor spoke softly, still feeling the hush of the night despite the growling of the Dobermans. He took his ID from his jacket pocket and held it up in front of him.

'Can't see it from here . . . means nothing . . . but where's Edwin?'

In the give of the light the woman revealed herself to wear short-cropped hair, have an angular, handsome rather than beautiful face, with high cheek bones and a small chin. She seemed to Ventnor to be in her mid-forties. She wore a silk gown with oriental patterning and slippers of soft leather. Her eyes were wide with fear and worry and apprehension.

'You are Mrs Hoole?'

'Yes.' She spoke with Received Pronunciation, as if she had been born into money or had socially climbed into it and had completed the necessary social adjustments. 'I was expecting Edwin.'

'Yes . . . I am afraid there's been an accident.' Ventnor continued to speak softly, as softly as he could, still feeling the night coldly and damply wrapping about him in what appeared to be a brief interlude between showers of heavy rain.

Somewhere behind the house an owl hooted.

'Oh . . .' The woman fell against the door frame and then rapidly collected herself and stood again. The dogs continued to eye and growl at Ventnor, totally focused. Very useful dogs, he conceded. A large house like Mirfield, remote, dark February night . . . yes . . . yes, very useful indeed, and especially for a woman alone. He realized then why the gateway of Mirfield was left open and why the driveway was of burglary friendly concrete and not of burglar unfriendly gravel, and why there were no security lights. Very useful dogs indeed. 'Can I take a closer look at your identification card, please?'

Ventnor stepped forward and held his warrant card closer to Mrs Hoole, allowing her to read it.

'Thank you, you'd better come in.' She turned to the dogs and said, 'Corner!' The dogs fell silent and turned and walked deeper into the hall. The door was shut, the chain slipped and then the door opened again.

Ventnor stepped over the threshold, adjusting his eyes to the light. The dogs sat together, side-by-side like two sentries in the corner of the hallway beside an internal door, between a hat stand and an umbrella stand, and continually fixed their eyes on Ventnor with a suspicious and aggressive stare.

'Don't worry about the dogs,' Mrs Hoole smiled. 'They won't attack you unless I tell them to do so, or unless you attack me, or even seem to threaten me in some . . . or in any way. So, just stay still and don't make any sudden movements, that is if you value your throat.'

Ventnor remained still. Very still.

'So what has happened?'

Ventnor told her. Mrs Hoole paled; she seemed genuinely concerned and said that she'd get dressed. Ventnor excused himself and said that if she didn't mind, he'd wait in the car. He liked dogs, but he also respected them and knew what a Doberman was capable of doing to someone who threatened their owner. They might subsequently be destroyed as dangerous dogs, but that would be of little compensation to him as he adjusted to life without a face, or was even in the clay. He didn't want to be left alone with two large and healthy males of the breed. His car was a sanctuary.

Mrs Hoole joined him in his car a few minutes later having dressed in some fetching but casual kit: jeans, a shoulder bag, leather jacket, long coat, boots. She left a security light burning and also clearly allowed the dogs free run within the house: Ventnor heard them both barking first in one room, then another. Once in the car she buckled

up as Ventnor reversed the vehicle gingerly down the
smooth driveway and into dark and dimly lit Workhouse
Lane.

'Can hardly see a damn thing if you reverse out,' Mrs
Hoole said matter-of-factly. 'That's why we tend to reverse
the cars in and that's why I knew it wasn't Edwin, I wouldn't
have seen Edwin's headlights on the curtains.'

'I see . . . quite practical.' Ventnor turned the car and drove
steadily towards the A64 York to Malton Road. The rain
began to fall relentlessly out of a low black sky.

'Well, my husband developed the practice and taught me
how to reverse for such a long distance; the driveway is
over one hundred feet long. I am Vivienne Hoole by the
way, and I am much younger than my husband.'

Ventnor didn't comment but he thought it a strange
thing to say, as though Vivienne Hoole was quite used to
being told that she looked much younger than her husband
or, as if vanity allowed her to think that was the case.
She was, after all, Ventnor was obliged to concede, very
attractive, and would have been a strikingly beautiful
young woman in her twenties, and still was possessed of
a figure that would be the envy of many twenty-year-
olds. He asked if she knew what her husband had been
doing in York.

Vivienne Hoole delved into her satchel-like shoulder bag
and extracted a packet of long cigar-like cigarettes. She
took one and lit it with a chunky-looking gold-plated lighter,
without asking for Ventnor's approval. She inhaled deeply
and exhaled through her nostrils. 'Ya.' She spoke needlessly
loudly in Ventnor's opinion. 'Ya, he was looking for his
brother.'

'His brother?'

'Ya, or rather an explanation.'

'An explanation—' Ventnor glanced at her – 'of what?'

Vivienne Hoole paused. She took another deep drag
on the cigar-long cigarette. 'I don't know the details.'
The smoke came out with her reply. 'You may as well
know that I am Edwin's second wife – he's my second
husband and I am his second wife. Edwin's first marriage

ended in a bloody and bitter divorce . . . very messy, it was like watching two animals fight to the death. I was on the distant touchline not really in his life until much later, so I wasn't the cause of the breakdown of the marriage.'

'I see.' Ventnor slowed for a large pool of water that had gathered on the road surface.

'Good,' she said, 'hit that too fast and it could cause a bad accident. But . . . oh ya . . . divorces can be messy or neat. Not been through one myself but I have observed plenty, I mean plenty, as if it has been my little life's lot . . . "not another divorce to walk someone through . . ." Well, Edwin's divorce was messy, blood and gore all over the landscape but I pieced that together over time, more from what he subsequently told me than from what I observed at the time. Edwin is a very private person. Even in marriage.'

'Even in marriage?' Ventnor's voice contained a note of shock and alarm.

'Yes. Why, does that surprise you?' She turned and smiled at him.

'No . . . it doesn't frankly.'

'Because of your occupation? You mean you have seen so many strange human situations that you are inured to all of it?'

'Well, yes, I dare say that is what I do mean. It's just the nature of the beast, but I don't find a person being private in marriage particularly strange but I didn't expect it to be the case in your household; it's always been a very working-class thing.' He paused as he took a difficult bend. 'I once met a family who didn't know what the husband and father did for a living. He just came home and dropped hard cash on the kitchen table and his wife wasn't permitted to ask where it came from.'

'That's not a marriage!' Vivienne Hoole snorted in dismay.

'Nope . . . less strange perhaps is that I have met individuals who are living with a deeply buried trauma that they will not share with their partner, or anyone, for that matter.'

Vivienne Hoole drew deeply on her cigarette. 'Yes, that sounds a bit like Edwin. He wouldn't keep me in the dark about anything I had a right to know but he wouldn't share everything with me. No secrets on a day-to-day basis, nothing like that, but it is as if the time before we met, that part of his life is his territory and the little woman must not trespass therein, that sort of privacy.'

'I see. So what is it that he is seeking an explanation about?'

'He is one of three brothers. I have met the other two, but like his first marriage, his relationship with them is something I am not allowed to be privy to.'

'Oh . . .' Ventnor stared at her briefly.

'But I do know that they are close to each other, very secretive and close, or were until his older brother died recently.'

'I see, sorry to hear that.'

'Natural causes, but it was the aftermath which apparently puzzled Edwin though I am not allowed to be fully aware of that, the little woman has her place and must remain in same but he has told me some of it, and I have overheard him talking on the phone to Leonard, his middle brother. Edwin is the youngest, then Leonard, then Harold . . . in ascending order . . . just four years between eldest and youngest, their mother produced one every two years. They grew up very close to each other. It is a very inward-looking family I have thought . . . it always seemed very incestuous on an emotional level. It seemed that all three wives were something to one side of their lives. At family gatherings these three would gravitate to each other and you couldn't drive a wedge between them. The point of this is that something puzzled Edwin about Harold's death, even thought it was natural causes . . . a massive stroke. Lucky dead I say, having met stroke victims who were dead lucky to survive . . . they thought.'

'I know what you mean.'

'But I don't know any details though I strongly suspect the issue of money is involved. It is a very materialistic family that I have married into.' She glanced out of the car window. 'Nearly a full moon,' she commented.

'Yes.' Ventnor stared straight ahead as the windscreen wipers swept from side to side. 'Still dark though . . . heavy cloud cover.'

'Too mild for February,' Vivienne Hoole commented softly, 'too wet and too mild. This just isn't February, not in the north of England anyway, maybe in the south, but not up here. Something is happening to the climate and I confess I don't like it . . . and the floods of late . . . it's all gone awry.'

'You notice that?'

'Anybody over forty will notice it.' She turned to him. 'You'll be too young. You'll think this is normal, you won't remember the hard winters . . . snowdrifts, railway lines and roads blocked for weeks on end. Whitby was cut off during one winter and the townsfolk were on the point of starving, they eventually got some food to them by sea. That was a particularly hard winter, but even so, this is spring-like.'

'Can't say I have ever known a hard winter, that I confess.' Ventnor shrugged. 'So, the money you mention?'

'Well—' Vivienne Hoole once again inhaled deeply – 'just brief and overheard snatches of conversation between Edwin and his brother Leonard, both deeply buried in said conversation, so deeply that Edwin dropped his guard and I was able to hear phrases like, "He just wouldn't do that, not Harold", and "He had no need of money, none at all", "We had a pact and Harold wouldn't have betrayed it, in fact it was his idea".'

'No details?'

'None, none that I was privy to and it wasn't my place to ask, anything that went on between the three brothers Hoole stayed with the three brothers Hoole.' She paused. 'Picture the scene, if you will, man and wife at home one evening, a quiet night in together . . . phone rings, man on phone to brother in the hall, door shut behind him for privacy from spouse, but voices become raised and so said spouse hears a little here and there, some whispered, so man does not completely forget spouse has ears. But spouse hears enough to work out that the late Harold Hoole did something so out of character that his death seemed suspicious to the two surviving brothers despite it being recorded as being of natural causes. It appeared to be something which came to light only after he died and which came as a huge, shocking surprise to Edwin and Leonard. Anyway, phone gets put down angrily and man comes and sits in his armchair and sits, heavily so. "Problems, dear?" wife asks consolingly, I am allowed to say that but not, "What is happening?", or "What was all that about?", otherwise I'd get my head bitten off, and husband growls something to the effect that it is nothing he "can't get to the bottom of", or that he "can't sort out", and that sort of phone call with that sort of content occurred numerous times and then man would pick up the morning's copy of the *Daily Telegraph* and open it and would hide behind it, signalling to the little woman that she must enquire no further. And certainly must not insist.'

'I see, well, as I said, if it makes you feel better, there was that family I once met . . .'

'Yes, at least it's not as bad as that, astounding that that woman tolerated it.'

'And seemed happy, that was the outstanding thing.' Ventnor drove on in silence and then asked. 'So, your brother-in-law might be the one to ask, it'll be some time before your husband will be able to be interviewed.'

'Yes . . . yes, Leonard is the man to ask and Edwin did go out in direct connection with "it", whatever "it" was or is, whatever "it" was that Harold did in breach of the pact.'

'Which was Harold's idea in the first place?'

'Apparently so, yes.'

'When did your husband leave the house?'

'In the late afternoon . . . yesterday. I thought you might be him returning unusually late until I realized that you were not reversing up the drive and until the dogs began to growl.'

'Yes . . . I thought that they'd be the sort of dogs you'd need if you lived in a house like that.'

'Yes, Cromarty and Tyne, excellent dogs.'

'Sea areas?'

'Yes.' Vivienne Hoole smiled. 'Edwin chose the names, he's an ex-Navy man.'

'What does he do now?'

'He digs the garden, plants vegetables, sits on various committees in the village.'

'Retired in other words?'

'Yes. He took fairly early retirement, not amazingly early, he was sixty. He worked as a financier for a finance company, Edwards and Edwards.'

'I haven't heard of it.'

'Corporate loans lending money to companies rather than to householders.'

'I see.'

'So, they advertise in trade publications but do not advertise on television. Nothing underhand, reasonable rates of interest, ethically defensive policy, not loan sharking or usury or anything of that manner, of that I am sure. I might have been sidelined in my marriage but my husband is a man of honour, he just has a Victorian attitude to marriage. He is a man of fair play, a church-goer. I would be devasteated if I found out otherwise. Devastated.'

'Is his surviving brother in the world of finance?'

'No, Leonard is a garage proprietor, quite upmarket and he values his reputation . . . fuel sales, servicing, repairs, the occasional second-hand car, but even then his second-hand cars are "born again". I mean stripped right back to essentials, engines rebuilt, parts replaced and fully serviced before he sells them, and for a modest profit. So safe that Edwin bought one for me, a small van, but very nice . . . just perfect for the little woman to go shop-ping in and take the dogs out for a long walk by the river, don't you think? He with his Jaguar and me with a little van, ex-Royal Mail, it's all she needs, but at least I know what he does for a living. The marriage you mentioned, extraordinary, no marriage at all. I will think of that for a long, long time.'

'What did your other brother-in-law do for a living?'

'Sold cameras.'

'Sold cameras?' Ventnor turned to her and smiled.

'Yes, YPR. He owned the chain.'

'Really?'

'Yes.' She returned the smile. 'Yorkshire Photographers Requisites, twenty shops in the chain, everything for the discerning photographer; cameras, accessories, film, used equipment but mainly new.'

'So all three were motivated by profit?'

'Yes . . . yes . . . you could say that but all three were gentlemen . . . two still are.'

Ventnor slowed as he entered the outer suburbs of York.

The larger man savagely punched the smaller man until he was semi-conscious. 'Pull yourself together,' he hissed. 'You're not going anywhere until you're together.' Then he punched him again, and again, and again, and continued smashing the smaller, younger man's face with his meaty fist long after the latter had lost consciousness.

'The birds are singing.'

Ventnor noticed how restrained she was as she made the observation. He thought her a little detached, but then, he reflected that her less than passionate marriage could perhaps explain her reaction. But even allowing for that Vivienne Hoole remained calm, not even wanting to sit down when the solemn-faced young surgeon broke the news to her. She had just stood still, perfectly still and said very calmly, 'I understand. Thank you.' She had turned to Ventnor and said, 'I want to go outside. Do you mind?' It was then, outside in the car park, still at the dead of night that she had commented, 'The birds are singing.'

'Yes,' Ventnor replied. 'Yes, they are.'

'Strange, don't you think?' She lit another of her clearly favoured long, dark cigarettes, and inhaled deeply.

A woman concerned about climate change, Ventnor thought, but not about her own health or risk to same.

'Strange? How so?'

'In that it's called the dawn chorus, but it's clearly still night, lacking fully two hours to dawn I should think, no sign of any daylight yet.' She glanced at her watch which she read in the spill of hospital lights. 'Four a.m., ten after really, but still nowhere near dawn.' She inhaled on the cigarette causing the tip to glow brightly in the shadows in which she and Ventnor stood. 'Well . . . so now I am a widow woman, widowed at forty-four. I did expect it. My mother . . . she buried two husbands . . . my mother told me to expect it. She said that when a woman gets married, she must then begin to prepare herself for widowhood. So I did expect it but just not this early in the piece . . .'

'Yes, I'm very sorry,' Ventnor spoke softly. Lights shone from the hospital and also from distant buildings and a ribbon of street lamps picked out the route of Wiggington Road, along which a night bus, empty of passengers, drove out of York.

'Hardly your fault,' she said with a smile, 'but thank you anyway. I dare say that in the end is the beginning, a new phase of life for me . . . a funeral to arrange, folk to notify, a new outfit to buy . . . black, and a wide-brimmed black hat with a veil of black lace. Edwin was always one for form and ceremony. I will also have to tell Cromarty and Tyne.'

'The dogs?'

'Oh yes, of course.' Vivienne Hoole turned to him and smiled. 'You have to tell the dogs. I will have them sit in front of me and talk to them. They will sense that not all is well, that something is amiss, they will notice Edwin's absence . . . they will feel it . . . and in time they will notice me getting rid of his things, parcelling them up to take to the charity shops.'

'Yes, in time. Can I ask you not to touch anything of his, please? This is a new murder inquiry.'

'Of course—' again she inhaled deeply – 'I wouldn't

move them for a while, not until a decent time has elapsed
and then offered to his family, they will have first refusal
of anything of his I do not want to keep. I am thinking in
terms of months but now not until the police say I can
dispose of them.'

'Thank you.'

'But the dogs will appreciate being told, it will make
them feel included . . . then I'll tell the frogs.'

'The frogs?'

'Oh, yes, the frogs must be told. We have . . . I have a
pond in the rear garden just inside the tree line, it has
frogs and newts. The newts are predators and eat the
frogspawn but we . . . I still hope to get a few frogs each
year. I have never felt any form of connection with the
newts, they're like Nile crocodiles, but I do feel an affinity
with the frogs and so I will sit by the pond and tell the
frogs. My father kept bees and it is the custom for bee-
keepers to tell the bees of any death in the keeper's family.
I extend the custom to the dogs and the frogs. I dare say
a psychologist will tell me I am really telling myself, it
is a way of accepting it, of coming to terms with it, but
I will still tell the dogs as soon as I return home and I
will tell the frogs later today after I have slept and during
the daylight. I will phone his brother immediately, of
course. I will get the priorities right – brother, dogs,
amphibians, but at least the birds have something to sing
about. Oh . . .' She pointed to the east.

'What is it?' Ventnor turned.

'Dawn.'

Ventnor saw a thin sliver of light like a finger probing
the darkness.

'On such nights, dawn comes to you like a mother.'
Viviene Hoole spoke slowly. 'The dawn brings a new beginning.' She dropped the cigarette onto the glistening wet
tarmac and ground it into lifelessness under her feet. 'So I
assume you wish to retain Edwin's clothing, that is the
clothing he was wearing when he was attacked?'

'Yes, we'll have to send them to the forensic science
laboratory at Wetherby, see what they can tell us. Every

contact leaves a trace, a hair fibre, a trace of DNA. A murder conviction can turn on such.'

'Yes . . . of course. So will you take me back to East Cowton please, Mr Ventnor? I have a couple of curious Dobermans that I have to explain things to and a phone call to make. Phone call, then dogs . . . then a widow's bed. That will be strange. That will indeed be strange.'

TWO

Tuesday, 9th February – 09.15 hours – 22.57 hours
*in which a family's secrets begin to unfold and George
Hennessey is at home to the gentle reader.*

Hennessey read the still slender file on the attack and
subsequent unlawful killing of Edwin Hoole, sixty-
six years, of East Cowton, Yorkshire. He then handed
it to Webster. 'Ventnor wrote it up to as far as he took it
before going home to get some well-earned sleep. Read it
please and then pick up the thread. You and DC Pharoah,
please.'

'Yes, sir.' Webster handed the file to Carmen Pharoah.

'Ventnor took it as far as he could, as you'll read. He
traced the CCTV footage. The deceased appears to have
walked, or staggered, with a serious head injury from the
Bishopthorpe area into the city where CCTV picked him
up at Skeldergate Bridge. That road leads out from York
over the motorway but doesn't connect to it.'

'No, sir.'

'And the deceased is known to be a motorist, a Jaguar
owner no less, yet he walked, a dying man, into York. So
it seems reasonable to assume that somewhere down that
road is a Jaguar, parked as if abandoned. We have to find
it. I'll get uniformed division on to that.'

'Sergeant Yellich?'

'Sir.' Yellich sat forward alert and attentive, cradling his
mug of tea in both hands.

'Can you please go and interview the wife of the
deceased? Ventnor got some information and he told her
that we'd be calling again.'

'Yes, sir.'

'So, Webster and Pharoah, please visit the brother of the
deceased, see what light can be shed, if any. At this stage
it still may have been a random attack with no motive other

than violence for its own sake. Mr Hoole might just have been in the wrong place at the wrong time . . . but . . . I don't know—' Hennessey glanced to his left at the walls of the city, at Micklegate Bar, glistening with rain under a low, grey sky; sullen, he thought, if the sky could have a mood it would be sullen – 'it just does not feel like a random attack and he did leave home to enquire, investigate something to do with, something in connection with, his brother's death. There were three brothers, you'll read, now just the one surviving. I don't want us to find out this was a premeditated murder when the trail has gone cold. No evidence yet to point to premeditation but it feels like it, it feels like it in my old copper's waters.'

'Understood, sir,' Yellich nodded. 'I know exactly what you mean, I really do. It does feel to be more than a wrong place and time number.'

'Good, pleased we are in agreement. OK with you two?'

'Yes, sir,' Webster repeated, as did Carmen Pharoah, both with equal enthusiasm.

'Good, pleased we are all of the same mind. So, we know what we are doing? Webster and Pharoah, you pay a call on Mr Leonard Hoole and Sergeant Yellich, Mr Hoole's relict. Back here at 14.00.'

'Yes, sir.'

The door of the house was opened slowly by a silver-haired lady with thin, firm-set lips and a face and eyes devoid of expression. It was, thought Webster, like being greeted by a robot. 'You'll be the police?' The woman spoke with a soft voice which had a trace of a north of England accent and which had also, he thought, a tone of world-weary resignation about it.

'Yes,' Webster replied, showing his ID, 'DC Webster . . . this is my colleague DC Pharoah.'

'Yes, you'll be here to see Leonard, my husband.'

'Yes, if he is at home.'

Mrs Hoole nodded. 'Yes, he's at home. I am Mrs Hoole, Mrs Muriel Hoole. Vivienne, icy lady at times, phoned us in the night, very matter-of-fact, to tell us that Edwin had been killed. Can't say that we have slept much since we got the call, we got up and made cocoa and sat or wandered about as if in a daze, like being in a dream, sitting in our dressing gowns until about nine a.m. when we got dressed. Oh, sorry, where are my manners? Keep you outside on a day like this? Please do come in.' Muriel Hoole stepped to one side to allow Webster and Pharoah ingress to her home. She closed the door gently behind them and said, 'Please, if you'll go into the living room, I'll tell Leonard that you are here, he's playing golf.'

'Playing golf?' Webster smiled as he entered what he found to be a neatly kept and pleasant-smelling living room, decorated strangely, yet to good effect in a blend of light and dark orange colours.

'Just an expression we use, it does amuse visitors and people who don't know us. Leonard is a keen golfer, he has rigged up a driving net at the side of the house, so he stands there whacking balls with all his might and they fly through the air for about fifteen feet before being arrested by the net and then fall harmlessly to the floor. He usually does that at the end of the day to unwind, he says that it is a lot healthier than stopping off at the pub for a few double gins. He's also got a hole in the lawn to practise putting, but right now he's whacking away, just lost his other brother, so he's whacking with all his strength. It's usually politic to leave him alone when he's driving but on this occasion. I think he'll want to talk to the police. Please do sit down, but not in that chair—' she pointed to a chair to the left of the fireplace – 'that's his. He's been venting long enough anyway, he'll be getting tired now but that's where he is, on the driving range, all fifteen essential therapeutic feet of it.'

'Thank you,' Webster said as Muriel Hoole left the room, walking with clearly practised poise and deportment.

Webster and Pharoah sat in deep, very comfortable chairs and silently read the room. It was, they both felt, just as one might expect of a couple of the Hoole's years, solid, expensive features, but done with taste and soothingly had many books in view. A small television set stood in the corner of the room, a small but powerful looking hi-fi system sat next to it. The carpet was of dark orange and deep pile. Prints of Pieter Bruegel the elder hung on the wall. The room did indeed say upon reading, 'successful businessman in his late fifties/early sixties, not known to the police', and upon which reading Reginald Webster and Carmen Pharoah began to relax, to feel at ease in their present surroundings.

Mr Leonard Hoole, when he entered the room just two or three minutes after Mrs Muriel Hoole taking her leave of the officers, revealed himself to be what Carmen Pharoah would think be best described as 'dapper', by which she always meant neatly turned out, meticulously smart with careful attention to detail of appearance, 'looking one's best' in a phrase. She also felt the word to mean brisk in movement and that too was Leonard Hoole as he strode into his living room much in the manner of an ex-serviceman, with his spine perfectly perpendicular. He wore highly polished brown shoes; grey cavalry twill trousers, a yellow casual shirt. He had a pencil line moustache and short, very short hair. 'Do, please sit down,' he said, as Pharoah and Webster made to rise as he entered the room. 'Sorry to have kept you . . . rum do.' He sat with full body control in 'his' chair. 'Very rum do. Just driving a few balls . . . I do that at certain times . . . dare say Muriel explained, and this is one of those times.'

'Yes.' Webster spoke for both himself and Pharoah. 'We are sorry to have to call in such circumstances.'

'Well, if the police knock on your door, or ring your doorbell, as in our case, they are not paying a call to tell you that you have won a fortune. Police calling means trouble, or a problem of some description.'

'Certainly for someone,' Carmen Pharoah said quickly, 'but not always for the person on whose door we knock. We could be seeking information, for example.'

'Aye.' Leonard Hoole seemed to the officers to glance into the middle distance and then refocus near at hand, 'but on this occasion it's trouble for us. First it was Harold, now it's Edwin.'

'First it was Harold?' Reginald Webster asked.

'Yes, my eldest brother, Harold. He died recently, two years ago.'

'Oh . . .'

'Yes—' Leonard Hoole grimaced – 'and now it's Edwin, my second eldest brother, and if trouble comes in threes?' He fell silent, then asked, 'What happened? Vivienne wasn't very clear. She was shocked it seemed, but didn't betray any emotion, not over the phone. She didn't seem upset. I offered to drive out to see her but she said she was fine and she wanted "space", by which she meant she wanted to be by herself for a while. Vivienne goes in for these therapy groups and has developed phrases like, "centering herself", "creative visualization". Don't know what she means but I have learned that by "space" she means she wants to be by herself, so she got "space". But me and Muriel sat up all night after she phoned. You can't sleep after you have news like that, not just before dawn but all Vivienne would say was that the circumstances of Edwin's death were suspicious. She wouldn't be drawn, which was annoying for us. But what happened? Do you know?'

'We know very little. Your brother was found by the police surgeon who attended to have sustained head injuries but at that time he was still alive. My colleague who attended recorded that your brother's pulse was so weak that it was barely detectable, even by the police surgeon. He was rushed to hospital but never regained consciousness. He had suffered a subdural haematoma.'

'Oh . . .' Leonard Hoole drew breath between his teeth. 'I have heard of that, very nasty, painless, but very nasty. Maybe it's a blessing. If he had survived he would have had massive brain damage, been like a stroke victim; paralysis, slurred speech . . . incontinent. Edwin would not have wanted that and Vivienne couldn't have coped with it. She crosses the road to avoid handicapped people, she wouldn't have been able to manage if her husband needed feeding like an infant and she had to empty his commode four or five times a day. So, maybe it was better this way. Vivienne said he was found well after midnight?'

'Yes. CCTV has him walking, making his way over the

Skeldergate Bridge in the early hours, towards the city centre.'

'On foot! Never! Edwin drove everywhere, or he'd take a taxi. He was a keen golfer like me but that was all the exercise he took, a round of golf once or twice a week and then only in the summer. I often used to tell him to take more exercise and he'd always say, "That's rich, you repair and service cars for a living and you tell me to walk. Ha!" So that's Edwin, he never went far without his car and not at the dead of night. He wouldn't have gone to York without his car, not from East Cowton. What on earth was he doing?'

'Well, that's what we hope you can help us with, sir. If you know what he was doing there, and at that hour, we'd be on our way.'

'On your way?'

'To solving the case,' Webster explained.

Hoole glanced at Webster. 'Solving the case? You don't think he was just set on, just attacked? What's the word . . . "mugged"?'

Webster opened his right palm in a gesture of ignorance. 'We don't know, but we don't think so. He wasn't mugged, that is certain, his wallet and his wristwatch were not stolen. Younger people tend to be victims of racist attacks and he was not in, or seemed to be coming from a dangerous area and so we can't close our minds to the notion of premeditated attack. We can't close our minds to anything. Mrs Hoole . . . Mrs Vivienne Hoole, that is, told us that she believed that her husband was meeting someone or going somewhere to find out about his brother Harold.'

'About Harold?'

'Yes. Do you know what she might have meant by that?'

Leonard Hoole sat back in his chair and said, 'Oh', and once again seemed to be looking into the middle distance. 'Oh,' he said again.

'If you know anything . . .' Webster began, but was silenced by Leonard Hoole raising his hand as if to say 'wait a moment, please.'

'My brother's death . . . that is Harold's death—' Leonard

Hoole spoke softly and slowly – 'there was something strange about it, something that just didn't add up.'

'Really?' Webster probed.

'Yes, the death itself, that was a stroke. Talking of strokes as we were, a massive brain haemorrhage, nothing suspicious there . . . but . . . upon a closer look things did in fact seem strange. Very strange indeed. What's that expression? Out of character? Yes, that's it, wholly out of character.'

'Really?'

'Well . . . yes.' Hoole paused and looked down at the carpet. 'In the first place there was the question of his will. You see we learned upon his death, at the reading of the will that he had released all the equity in his house. You will have seen adverts on television inviting people to do that.'

'Yes,' Webster replied, 'they make it look so inviting. Damn stupid thing to do, if you ask me, especially if you have children and want them to inherit something, give them a financial leg up in life.'

'That's the way I feel about it. You don't want pots of money in the lag end of life to go on holidays you don't really enjoy. For me, people of our age want the security of home ownership, enough money to sustain the lifestyle they wish and the comfort of the knowledge that they are going to leave their children a property to inherit. It is for them to release the equity after you have passed on. Heavens, who wants to go to Rio de Janeiro when you're in your sixties or seventies? I am in my sixties and I never want to leave these shores again. I have seen sufficient of the world to know where I want to be and it isn't overseas and all of my friends feel the same. Really, I know of no one who'd want to spend their children's inheritance. I mean, who'd prune the apple trees?'

'Your brother, Harold thought like that?' Webster asked. 'He was of the same mindset, of the same attitude?'

'Oh, yes, and Edwin also. In fact all three of us, as well as our friends, used to scoff at such adverts on television. You've earned your retirement and should enjoy it. Indeed, well, yes, we have earned our retirement and we are enjoying it thank you very much and a huge part of that enjoyment is in owning our own homes. Take that away and there's not a lot of security left for a silver-haired man or woman or couple. You might be able to live in your house until you expire but it isn't yours any longer. It's owned by the finance company.'

'Indeed.'

'I just wouldn't sleep at night, knowing that I had signed over the ownership of my house after years of working to pay off the mortgage. It just wouldn't be the same roof over my head.'

'Indeed,' Webster repeated, 'but you say that is what Harold did?'

'Yes.' Hoole snapped the reply as if still in some form of denial. 'That was what he did and what makes it all so very strange. It was wholly out of character. You see we three grew up learning the value of home ownership. It was instilled into us that rent is dead money and to 'buy land, because they don't make it anymore'. My father always used to tell us to strive to own our own homes. He owned his and so did his siblings. I mean, nothing fancy just lower-middle-class inter-war three-bedroomed semi-detached houses, those sort of houses, but it was theirs. All our cousins got mortgages straight away and in the fullness of time they inherited their parents' house, as we did. It was just the attitude of the family, and also of the whole extended family.'

'I understand,' Webster said softly. 'I get the picture, I get it very clearly.'

'So we grew to be middle-aged men and instead of attending weddings we started to attend funerals and then gather for the reading of wills to learn of the money coming our way. The sale of my father's home raised money which we three brothers shared equally and it all went to reduce our mortgage commitments and my money will go to my children in exactly the same way. I will feel that my life will have been worth something if I leave something. It is the steady accumulation of wealth that appeals to me. They will inherit this house and a thriving business, more than I inherited from my father, but they will leave their children more than I will leave them, perhaps expand the garage into a string of garages like Harold extended his camera shop into a string of shops. That, you see, Mr Webster and Miss Pharoah that is the attitude of the Hooles.'

'Yes.'

'Clearly so,' added Carmen Pharoah. 'Very clear . . . the Protestant work ethic.'

'Yes,' Hoole nodded, 'that's a good way of putting it. I like that, the Protestant worth ethic. So, as I said, with that background it came as a huge shock to find out that Harold had released all the equity in his home some years before he died. It was so alien that at the time I thought it was like being part of a staunch Orange family in Northern Ireland to find that your brother had converted to Catholicism, but only finding that out upon his death. That was the depth of the shock.'

'I see.' Webster paused and then asked, 'What were relationships like within his family?'

'Warm and healthy so far as I could tell. I knew of no squabble that would make Harold want to disinherit his sons. In fact if that had been the case, Harold would have just done that, had his will redrafted to exclude one or both and told them he had done so. He just would not have sold out to one of those "you deserve to enjoy your retirement outfits" . . . but he did.'

'I understand that, Mr Hoole, Mr Harold Hoole, was a widower?'

'Yes and he didn't have anyone else in his life at the time of his death. No lady companion found in the personal columns of Saga magazine, just himself. He seemed content at the time.'

'How did he lose his life?'

'Stroke, as I said. No one was present when he suffered it. His body was discovered by his son, Keith, his eldest. Harold didn't answer the midday phone call that his son always made to check on him, so Keith called round and found his father slumped in the armchair. No sign of a break-in or of any theft. He had gone to sleep in his chair, in front of the television and that—' Hoole paused again, as if searching for words – 'was also a little strange, again out of character.'

'Oh?'

'Yes. Harold hated daytime television, loathed it. He had no time at all for folk who sit and soak it up and people with all those satellite dishes and aerials attached to the house so they can access fifty channels twenty-four seven. He was always so scathing of such folk. "Get out and enjoy the day" was his motto, "Go out and have a long walk . . . just get out . . . no matter what the weather is like, don't sit and vegetate in front of a TV screen, not at two o'clock in the afternoon on a summers day."'

'Yet that was what he was doing?'

'It appeared so . . . so it appeared, so we were told.' Leonard Hoole sighed. 'The post and the newspaper had been picked up that day and carried inside . . . and . . . oh yes . . . there was the yellow shirt.'

'The yellow shirt?'

'Yes, Harry wore a yellow shirt at times, not a yellow tee shirt or a woollen yellow overshirt like I am wearing but a full shirt. Confess we thought it looked a little silly, a man of his age, but he would wear it nonetheless. He took to doing so just before he died. He seemed to have recovered some zest for life. He suffered despondency for a while after his wife's death but latterly developed this youthful sort of attitude. You see, his attitude to growing old was to say that you are as young as you feel and so he began to dress in a loud, flamboyant fashion.'

'I see.'

'He tended to dress younger than his years and he'd go to the university.'

'The university?' Webster smiled.

'Yes, at Heslington; he'd wander on to the campus and walk round it. He'd walk into one of the cafeterias and buy a meal. No one bothered him; they would take him for a mature student or a member of the teaching staff, or a university employee, but Harold's eyes would be working, scanning left and right like radar and he'd be eyeing up the girls, particularly the girls. But all that youth, all that enthusiasm, he explained to me once that it seemed to rub off on him. He would go to the university in the morning, spend a few hours there and leave in the mid-afternoon, saying he felt to be about twenty years old, not only in his body but also in his attitude. Seemingly he was like one of those dogs or cats that think they are human beings because that's all they see. It was in one of his regular wanderings into the university that he bought the yellow shirt from the campus shop, but the point being, he was seen wearing the yellow shirt the day before he died, but when he was found he was wearing a grey one, very middle-aged.'

'So, he hadn't been up all night?'

'Exactly. He had retired, gotten up quite normally, got dressed, picked up the post and the newspaper but did not open them.'

'He didn't open the mail?'

'No, nor did the newspaper appear to have been read but he didn't respond to his son's midday call and was found deceased in front of a switched-on television set at mid-afternoon.'

'Yes.' Webster spoke softly. 'I can see the inconsistencies.'

'Well, for a man who loathes daytime television, to switch the set on before opening his mail or reading his news-paper, a bit odd, don't you feel? Don't you think? We certainly thought so. Yet we know he had retired the previous night and so hadn't left the television on all night. He wouldn't do that, he was very cautious, very safety-minded, conscious of the dangers of not switching a television set off at night. It just does not add up. And the weather . . . it was during the summer, a lovely summer's day, on such a day Harold would be at the university watching the girls in their summer frocks and tee shirts. He'd return home like a frisky colt and be in the Waggoner's Arms for a few beers. There was, though, nothing that said "suspicious circumstances" to the police. So many sixty-year-olds sit in front of the television during the day, so many sixty-year-olds have strokes, but you knew, if you knew his lifestyle, if you knew his attitude, it just didn't make sense

and then upon his death we found out he had sold his house
to a finance company who had allowed him to remain living
there but they had possession of the deeds. It is so very
strange.'

'The money?' Webster asked. 'Do you know what
happened to that?'

'From the sale of the house?'

'Yes.'

'Oh . . . all accounted for. Some had been spent but the
majority was in the bank, in a deposit account, so he'd done
the sensible thing there. His sons did inherit something, but
nothing like the value that the house was upon his death
because of the recent boom in the housing market. In the
five years between the selling of the house and Harry's
death, the house doubled, nearly tripled in value.'

'He kept it from everyone that he had sold the house . . .
for five years?'

'Yes, he kept it very, very quiet but in fairness that is
another Hoole family characteristic, we have always played
our cards very close to our chests, just a long-standing family
trait.' Leonard Hoole glanced up at the ceiling and then drew
a deep breath. 'He was a recent widower at the time he sold
his house and like I said, he took his wife's death very badly.
I have wondered if his mind just wasn't where it should have
been, if he was vulnerable to the hard sell. Perhaps that's
why he kept quiet; he might have regretted what he had done.
He certainly didn't spend the money and it's hardly worth
releasing the equity unless you are going to spend it. In fact
there is no point at all in doing so.'

The door opened, Mrs Muriel Hoole entered carrying a
mug of tea on a tray which she handed to her husband.
'Are you sure I can't get you two anything?' She smiled at
the officers.

'No, thank you.' Carmen Pharoah shook her head, also
smiling.

'As you wish.' Muriel Hoole withdrew quietly, shutting
the door behind her.

'So—' Webster picked up the thread of the interview –
'your brother's body was found by his son, Keith?'

'Yes, as I said.'

'Alright, we'll have to talk to him. Where can we find him?' Leonard Hoole gave an address in York.

'Did you express concerns about your brother's death?'

'No—' Hoole sipped his tea – 'we didn't. I think we were too close to it at the time. There didn't appear to be any suspicious circumstances, not immediately, we were all stunned by his death. He was very fit, not a stroke material man at all. The police line was natural causes and we accepted it and one of my employees had died of a stroke a few weeks beforehand and he was only thirty-five . . . and so because of that our attitude was well, "such things happen".'

'I understand.' Webster nodded. 'Can we ask about Mrs Hoole, Harold's wife?'

'Laura?'

'Is that her name? Yes. You said she had died a few months earlier.'

'Yes, just about six months earlier. They were very close, it was a successful union. They were very happy which is why I think Harry must not have been himself when he did what he did and released all his equity. He did just not give informed consent . . . but Laura, her death was a tragedy but wholly accidental. You might have read about it, as a so-called "joyrider" had stolen a car and lost control of it, left the road and ran into Laura. She was killed instantly. She was in the wrong place at the wrong time.'

'In York?'

'Yes, on Tadcaster Road, about five or six years ago. That was the first tragedy in our family.' Hoole paused. 'Then five years of normaley and then my two brothers die within a few months of each other. We are a strong family but everyone can be worn down. I don't think I could take another blow at the moment, I couldn't handle it.'

'We hope you won't have to, sir.'

'I hope so as well.' Hoole smiled.

'So . . .' Carmen Pharoah asked, 'was Edwin divorced or widowed . . . or late marrying? What was his situation?'

'Divorced, he was taken to the cleaners. His house at East Cowton on Workhouse Lane, have you seen it?'

'No, neither of us have.'

'Well, it's impressive but modest compared to his earlier house. Edwin's success came despite his first wife, not because of it. She had her own business as well. She didn't deserve half the turkey when it came to carving-up time but the laws, the divorce laws, they swing like a pendulum. They used to favour the male, now they favour the female. I dare say in a few years' time they'll be redrafted to favour the male. I was talking to a solicitor at the golf club about this just the other day and he said the divorce laws we have now have probably saved the life of a lot of men.' Hoole smiled. 'What he meant was that the divorce laws at the moment so strongly favour the wife that women don't have to grease the stairs or hire thugs to bump off their errant husbands. They just need to sue for divorce and they are guaranteed half the property. Not bad.'

Pharoah and Webster shared the joke by also smiling.

'But all joking aside, if a woman is ruthless enough she can do very well out of her divorce. And Edwin's wife was sufficiently ruthless.'

'Really?'

'Oh, yes . . . Ruth by name but ruthless by nature.'

'And she was self-employed?'

'She was a certified accountant, not as full blown and of the status of a chartered accountant but she could earn a reasonable crust for herself by guiding folk through our maze of tax laws. She did well for herself. She also knew a lot about the divorce laws, so she acquired half the value of a lovely old Victorian house with acres of land, half of Edwin's stocks and shares portfolio, half the capital he had and she also forced a generous maintenance allowance for herself. So Vivienne came into his life like a breath of fresh air. She has a good quality of life but she didn't marry him for his money, that's for sure.'

'Where is Ruth now?' Webster asked. The woman was beginning to interest him.

'In the Yellow Pages, Ruth de Vries, certified accountant.

She retained her maiden name for business purposes. Mind you, she could be retired now . . . she's certainly acquired enough money,' Hoole added with a growling menace to his voice.

'I think I'd like to chat to her.' Webster glanced at Carmen Pharoah who nodded in agreement.

There was then a lull in the conversation, broken by Webster who asked, 'Did you and your brother Edwin come to discuss your brother Harry's death? I mean your suspicions about it?'

'Yes . . . yes, we did latterly so, in the last few weeks. We agreed that things were deeply suspicious but as I said, we both agreed that they just didn't add up. We both felt ill at ease about it but equally, we thought we had insufficient cause to go to the police.'

'Did Edwin tell you who he was meeting?'

'No. If he had done so, I would have liked to have gone with him—' Hoole once again glanced up towards the ceiling – 'and that is strange as well come to think of it . . .'

'Oh?'

'He would have kept it from his wife, the Hoole characteristic, but he would have shared it with me. I would have expected him to do so anyway, so he probably didn't place too much store in it, whatever "it" was. There is that to consider.'

Edwin Hoole's Jaguar was located close by Warren Pond on the Bishopthorpe Road, in an open area of flat meadowland beyond the bypass, near the river and also near to the outlying Bishopthorpe suburb. The car was parked, neatly so, rather than carelessly abandoned, and looked to Hennessey as though there was nothing about the vehicle which might arouse suspicion, except perhaps that the location of the car was a little isolated, and as such would invite the attention of car thieves and teenage vandals. If the vehicle had still been there in twenty-four hours' time then a good and conscientious beat patrol officer would have reported it as a suspect stolen car. But other than that, it was a parked Jaguar, in striking red, what Hennessey understood to be known as Italian racing red, the blood-red colour associated with Ferraris. Perhaps a little upmarket for Bishopthorpe, but other than that it was a parked car, no discernible damage, about two years old and an all-round very nice bit of kit.

George Hennessey, being the only available CID officer available when the finding of the sought-for vehicle was reported, attended the scene. He observed for the CID, as fingerprints were taken from the door and boot handles, and further observed as the driver's side door was forced to allow the vehicle to be loaded on to a trailer to be towed to the forensic science laboratory at Wetherby for testing and analysis.

George Hennessey pondered the scene, walking from where Edwin Hoole's Jaguar had been parked out for a hundred yards and then back to the car, and walked out again in another direction for another hundred yards, searching the ground for any clue as to what might have happened, looking for the spoor of any scuffle for example, searching for anything which he felt might be relevant but he detected nothing that might be of relevance, no scuffed soil, no murder weapon, nothing indeed to say that where the car was parked was even a crime scene. Whoever Edwin Hoole had met there, if anyone, whoever had driven him away in their car, if anyone, had not left any recognizable trace of their presence or identity. A mile, Hennessey guessed, as he glanced at the road, a mile for Edwin Hoole to walk from there to where he had collapsed in wet, dark Spurriergate, collapsing in a mound that a constable first thought were two plastic refuse bags. It was a long, long way for a man to stagger who knew that he was seriously injured, possibly even knew he was fatally injured and had to reach hospital if he had any hope of survival, but yet in his shock was not able to think of asking for help, knocking on a door, phoning from a telephone kiosk, in deep shock, just focused on reaching the safety of York District Hospital. If indeed he was attacked or abandoned near his vehicle. Such fear he must have felt within the sense of shock, such loneliness, such vulnerability in the rain, yet perhaps the rain refreshed him and enabled him to go further than he would have been able to walk had the weather been of the type of Februarys Hennessey recalled from his now distant childhood and young adulthood; Februarys of ice and snow and sleet. Nonetheless it would have been a long, dark, dimly lit road for a dying man to walk, and cruelly, cruelly unjust and any passing motorist might have presumed him drunk and driven on, rather than stopping to render what might have been life-saving assistance. Open fields close by and any lights would be distant as Edwin Hoole put one foot in front of the other, striving to reach his destination. Not, thought Hennessey, not a pleasant end to any life. A curlew caught his eye, swooping low out of the still, grey sky, and landing confidently and gently in the meadow at the far side of the flat, ice cold river.

Life was going on.

'They know.' Vivienne Hoole sat in a black and red Oriental housecoat and comfortable-looking slippers. She sipped a cup of tea. 'The dogs, Cromarty and Tyne.' She nodded to the two Dobermans who sat together in the corner of the room, each fixing Yellich with a watchful gaze. 'You must not underestimate them. I told them about Edwin, I told them that he wasn't coming home anymore and you could see it in their eyes, they knew . . . believe me, they knew.'

'Yes.' Yellich sipped the tea that had been pressed into his hand by an emotionally restrained Mrs Hoole, but who, he thought, could not fully hide her appreciation of human company. 'I understand that . . . I have heard that about Dobermans and also the same of other breeds, very astute creatures.'

'Yes, astute is the very word. I also told the frogs as dawn was fully breaking . . . I saw the beginning of today, well, the beginning of the daylight hours, from the car park outside the hospital, just a sliver of light in a black sky and by the time I got home and had told the dogs it was quite light and so I walked into the garden, the rear garden and told the frogs.' She sipped her tea. 'I understand why they tell the bees.'

'The bees?'

'Yes,' she smiled briefly. 'As I explained to the other officer, Mr . . . Mr . . . holiday resort in the Isle of Wight . . . help me . . .'

'Ventnor.'

'Yes, thank you, Mr Ventnor, very pleasant young man. As I explained to him I grew up in rural England and when someone dies, it is the custom for a relative of the deceased to tell the bees. They don't produce honey unless they are told of someone's passing – just a country folk superstition but when I was telling the frogs, I was also telling myself. I was accepting Edwin's death. I now see the importance of telling the bees.'

'Thank you.' Yellich smiled. 'Interesting.'

'Yes, I learned why my father went down the garden path and sat next to the beehive for an hour or so as though he was talking to himself . . . on the day his brother died . . . talking away with his head buried in his hands. In just the same way I sat next to a pond telling the water about Edwin. Didn't see a frog, wrong time of year and the richest thing is there probably isn't any frogs in there anyway, not since Edwin brought the damn newts back. He did that last summer and released them in the pond. We learned too late that those ferocious little beasts eat frogspawn. Can't talk to a newt like you can talk to a frog, frogs have a certain quality about them, their eyes look at you . . . they seem to have a character . . . newts don't . . . and there's something honest about a frog, sitting there so still . . . newts dart about like thieves in the night. Sorry, I ramble.'

'I can return if you'd like to rest? It's been a long night for you.'

'No—' she inclined her head in gratitude – 'no, I had a nap after talking to the pond. I had just gotten up when you called. First time I have awoken as a widow. That bed will always be a bit on the large side for me now. I'll let the dogs have his pillowcase and a pair of his unwashed socks, something with his scent on them.'

'Difficult.'

'Have you been bereaved?'

Yellich shook his head. 'No, no I haven't . . . not anyone close to me at least . . . just grandparents and I wasn't particularly close to them, so no one really close. I still have both parents, wife and a son, all alive and well. So I dare say the experience of bereavement is ahead of me.'

'Ahead of you, as you say. It's only when your parents die that you truly realize the actuality of your own mortality and life becomes more precious . . . but Edwin. I am sorry I wasn't able to be very helpful this morning.'

'Understandable, it's why I was asked to call on you later. So you indicated to Mr Ventnor that he was going to meet someone?'

'Yes. Edwin was concerned about the death of his brother Harold who died about eighteen months ago, probably a little more. I'm afraid I don't know all the details of the reason for his suspicion. His surviving brother, Leonard, will help you there I am sure.'

'That's alright. As we speak, two of my colleagues are visiting him.'

'Ah, well, the three . . . then two . . . then one . . . they don't share . . . didn't share much, put a strain on our marriage but Edwin didn't think that Harry's death was as natural as it seemed. As I said to Mr Ventnor, I just over-heard the occasional phone call . . . or Edwin's half of the occasional phone call. Then—' she paused – 'then he took a phone call . . . seemed to have significance for him.'

'When was that?'

'Two . . . three weeks ago. It clearly puzzled him, sent him away brooding. We have not been long married but I have lived with him long enough to know that that phone call troubled him.'

'But there was a time span, a period of two or three weeks before he left to meet someone? Was the phone call you mention significant, do you think it was somehow relevant to his death?'

'I have no way of knowing. It might have been about some other matter . . . there may also have been other calls which came when I was out of the house. I am normally out of the house during the afternoon, attending to one thing

or another, or else in the gym. I like to keep trim and in
as good a shape as I can. I am no female bodybuilder but
weights work well for me . . . as does the occasional run . . .
but it's safer in the gym.'

'Safer?'

'Oh, from attack, a woman cannot jog alone without some
attendant risk . . . there is no such risk in the gym.'

'Of course, I was a bit slow there—' Yellich forced a
smile – 'especially for a police officer.'

'So there is no way of telling if other phone calls were
received when I was not at home and Edwin would not
have shared them with me anyway.'

'Secretive, as you said.' Yellich glanced quickly round
the room, half drawn velvet curtains were keeping the room
in a low and gentle light, solid, expensive-looking
furniture, books on shelves on the wall, indeed similar to
the décor that Webster and Pharoah were observing in
Leonard Hoole's home. 'What was your late husband's
demeanour, his manner like in the last two or three weeks?'

'Quiet, come to mention it, quieter than normal I would
say but only in hindsight does that seem relevant. He was
abnormally quiet. He could be moody, be withdrawn for
weeks on end, so his broody attitude in the last days of his
life didn't seem too unusual . . . but then, as I said . . . in
hindsight . . . but he more or less carried on as normal,
played golf, went out in the evenings . . .'

'Any mail of note? Anything like that?'

'Again, not that I know of. The post is delivered late here,
sometimes after midday, and it is mostly junk, as all mail
seems to be.'

'Yes—' Yellich spoke softly – 'all the important stuff is
sent by email or fax.'

'So the collection of the post is, or was, delegated to
the little woman—' Vivienne Hoole pointed to herself –
'but if he happened to be near the front door when the
stuff came through the letter box he was not above kneeling
down and scooping it up. So again, I can't be a hundred
per cent sure that something of significance was not
delivered by Steve, the postman.'

'I see.' Yellich paused and once again glanced at the room, at the high, beamed ceiling and the potted plants along the window ledge. 'Sorry, but I am grasping in the dark here. It's difficult to see at the moment what is and/or is not relevant.'

'I quite understand.' Her smile seemed warm and genuine.

'You say that you are his second wife?'

'Yes, no shame there. Second best, as they say.'

'None at all.'

'Especially since he is my second husband,' she explained. 'So we came to each other as used goods but also both determined to make this union work. That's what we told each other.'

'Good.'

'But I felt, I confess, I felt that I gave more than I received. I think I tolerated his secretiveness more that I should have done. I should have kicked up more of a fuss . . . I mean about sharing. I tended to be—' she drew breath and looked to her left for a second or two – 'well, I was going to say that our marriage was a one-way street but that is an over-statement, though there was an imbalance in the giving. It was perhaps more like a motorway where there is a contraflow . . . so four lanes in one direction and two in the other, with my giving being the four lanes, his being the two, if you see what I mean. Sorry, I think in images, but I contented myself with the situation because I was deter-mined to make the marriage work and I believe I was successful . . . I can say that. I am a widow, I am not a twice-over divorcee.'

'I see, well, good for you. So, tell me about the first, the previous Mrs Hoole.'

'One Ruth de Vries by name, the ice-maiden by nature. One very cold fish. We actually met once or twice. She is self-employed now in the same capacity as Edwin was . . . property or finance, or both . . . that sort of field, but as a person I knew very little about her and want to know little else. We are both men's women and so do not do well in each other's company. I certainly longed for some male company within a few moments of meeting her, and I sensed

that she felt the same . . . or perhaps it was just a mutual
dislike. On that occasion we were both dressed to kill and
were competing for the same prey . . . both of us were on
a determined testosterone hunt and so some friction was
going to be inevitable.'

'When was that?'

'Oh, some few years ago now . . . a function at the golf
club, that is the Heslington Golf Club. It always seemed to
me to be a more open version of the Masonic Lodge, but
if you are in business and in York, you need to be in the
HGC.'

'Yes, so I have heard. It does indeed have that reputation.'

'All above board, of course. York isn't a "brown envelope" town, at least not that I am aware and I have been
married into York commerce for over twenty years. My
first husband was . . . still is, a builder . . . a house builder
and Edwin was in finance, so both were in the "need-to-
know-the-right-person-club", and where do you meet the
right person but the HGC . . . but that is all very proper,
as I said. Unlike Hull which has a reputation for being
a "brown envelope town". My husband, my first
husband and I were divorced because of his infidelity
and so being insincere was something he was capable
of. His secretary was also his mistress for a long time.
No wonder he came home late at night and too tired to
give any attention to me.'

'Sorry to hear that.'

'Well, that's life . . . but one day he drove home from a
business meeting in Hull looking very ashen-faced and said,
"I can't do business in that town", and never went to Hull
again, not on business anyway. You must know of him,
Henry Alcock . . . Alcock homes . . . new build housing
estates. You see the signs everywhere.'

'Oh, yes, building on the flood plain. Brave of him.'

'Yes. The land is guaranteed to flood so he is putting them
on metal stilts, five feet high solid metal girders in a bed of
concrete to raise the houses above the flood waters and provide
storage space beneath the living area for things which can't
be water damaged; garden tools, for example. The drive is

elevated so the family car will be safe and each house will be provided with a small fibreglass dingy, so it will be equipped when the floods come but the floods will not come each year and then they will only last a few days at a time. So he's doing well there. Anyway, Ruth de Vries, she and I met at the golf club, and still do from time to time and we talk, on a superficial basis only. Strange, I seem to know more about my ex-husband than I know about my late husband.'

'Can we return to yesterday?'

'Conversation-wise you mean?' Vivienne Hoole smiled. 'Yes, we can. I am sorry I wandered. Of course.'

'What time did your husband leave the house in order to rendezvous with said person or persons unknown?'

Vivienne Hoole paused and glanced at the carriage clock which sat upon the mantelpiece. She turned to Yellich. 'At a strange time.'

'Oh?'

'Yes . . . about five p.m. It was a strange time for him, he is usually settling in for the evening about then, or arriving home, not leaving and five p.m. is a strange time for anybody to leave the house for a period of time. I mean there's the traffic for one thing. Why leave just in time to encounter the rush hour?'

'Why, indeed?'

'He rushed away . . . well Edwin didn't rush in the eyes of everyman, he had a slow, deliberate way of moving, but for him it was rushed. He didn't say goodbye or tell me when to expect him home which he usually did . . . which he normally would have done and for Edwin that was a hurried departure.'

'So, anxious to go somewhere, anxious to meet someone and all in connection with the death of his brother Harold some eighteen months ago?'

'Yes.' Vivienne Hoole drained her cup of tea and placed it in the saucer with a noticeable 'clink'. 'That really sums it up neatly, very neatly indeed.'

George Hennessey thought Louise D'Acre looked troubled. He said so.

Dr D'Acre responded by shooting him a disapproving glare and then rapidly looked away.

'Sorry . . .' Hennessey mumbled and looked around her cramped office, the photographs of her children, three – two teenage girls and a pre-teenage boy, and of Samson, her magnificent black stallion.

'No—' she put her hand up to her forehead – 'it's just a guilt trip. I did something I probably shouldn't have done, and something I regret doing and just don't know what to do now.'

Hennessey remained silent.

'It's a real tragedy.' Dr D'Acre looked at the photographs of her children. 'It's my friend's son, just twenty-two years old, a few years older than Fiona my eldest, he and his friends went to Tunisia recently for a bit of winter sun. My friend implored them to remain in Europe but he and his friends were dead set on setting foot on the African continent . . . the Dark Continent—' she grimaced – 'young men and their thirst for adventure. Anyway, Stefan, my friend's son . . . his father is Polish you see . . . and he took her name upon marriage so that their children would have the British-sounding name of Henderson, but gave their three boys Polish Christian names, Zoltan, Ivan and Stefan. Anyway, Stefan got separated from his friends one night in Tunis. His friends reported him missing to the police but they couldn't, or wouldn't do anything. A few days later his body was found, naked, floating in the sea and the post-mortem found two small cuts on his ankles at the artery and not a drop of blood in the body.'

'Oh,' George Hennessey groaned.

'Yes.' Louise D'Acre held eye contact with Hennessey. 'He'd been mugged for his blood. Eight pints of good, healthy blood to sell to a hospital in Tunis . . . or somewhere . . . no questions asked. You know, I find it astounding that any hospital could buy blood without questioning its provenance, but someone, or some intermediary agency . . . it would probably have gone through a middleman who led the hospital to believe that they were buying lawfully donated blood, but no checking could have been done, no documentation of authenticity, nothing. Stefan's body was returned to the UK and his parents collected it from Manchester Airport and brought it back to York. Well, they had it brought back, the protocol of handling the deceased being what it is.'

'Yes.'

'They asked me if I would look at the body. They wanted to know if I could tell if he was conscious. They wanted to know if he knew what was happening to him, if I could find any evidence of him being unconscious ... like a head injury ... that would be of some crumb of comfort.'

'And?'

'I could find no such indication. In fact there is indication of fear, there was bruising to both wrists, suggesting restraint and of the extent I would expect to find if the person was struggling against said restraint, not commented on by the Tunisian pathologist. He or she might have missed it because the skin was tanned. He got his winter sun alright; he went missing just before the end of the holiday. He might even have been targeted in advance and lured into a honey trap, we'll just never know, but whether the Tunisian pathologist missed or ignored the bruising as being irrelevant to the cause of death, the fact remains that the evidence of forcible restraint, and struggle against the restraint indicates, nay all but proves, consciousness at the time of insanguination.'

Hennessey again groaned. 'How awful.'

'It bears not thinking about, being conscious as your blood is slowly drained away, gradually feeling weaker and colder and eventually a little light-headed, knowing you are dying, aged twenty-two, in a foreign country surrounded by people who were killing him, watching him die and perhaps one was the dusky, dewy-eyed maiden who was the bait in the honey trap, just coldly taking his life. The sense of betrayal he must have felt. I knew him all his life ... I remember him teething, remember him going to school for the first time ... his birthday parties, the joy at his degree, a two-one from Newcastle.'

'Not bad.'

'Very not bad . . . all that future ahead of him, the doors that were opening for him with a two-one. Now he's in a drawer in the next room.' Dr D'Acre tapped a slender finger on the wall beside her. 'I think I will tell my friends that I could find no evidence of him being conscious.' She leaned back in her chair, a balanced female face, no make-up save a trace of pale, almost transparent lipstick, hair short in a 'boy cut' style so-called. She glanced at Hennessey and then at her compact desk top which afforded, so Hennessey had always thought, a ridiculously small working surface and then said, 'Or perhaps, what harm will it do if I said that I detected petechial haemorrhaging in the eyes which would indicate partial suffocation, or traces of ether in his nostrils, enough to cause brain death. That can be done in sixty seconds, but it would not stop the heart from beating. I think I will tell them that. I think it would be what I wanted to hear if I was in their shoes and I will take my actual findings with me to my grave, share them with no one else.'

'It's unlikely that we will become involved in his murder, but I will do the same.'

'I appreciate that; you might meet them one day.' She smiled but avoided eye contact. 'So what do we have, any developments?'

'Well, yes.' Hennessey leaned backwards in the upright chair on which he sat having become aware that he had leaned forward as Louise D'Acre had related the terrible tale of the death of her friend's son and of her findings in respect of his death. 'We have determined his identity, wholly so . . . no question.'

'Yes, his wife, now his widow was at the hospital when he died, so I believe?'

'Yes, that is the case.'

'And the casualty doctor has recorded his belief that death was caused by a subdural haematoma, very unpleasant, pointless, and like my friend's son, the victim is conscious and possibly has some insight into what is happening but is unable to communicate, knowing that he is fatally injured and being unable to communicate said fact. Often such victims are dismissed as drunks.'

'So I have heard, ma'am. In fact we believe Mr Hoole was attempting to reach hospital when he collapsed. We have CCTV footage of him making his way in the direction of the hospital and indeed he is staggering from side to side as if drunk.'

'Classic symptoms of SDH, drunken-like behaviour but not aggressively so. So—' she closed the notes sent from York District Hospital Accident and Emergency Department – 'we seek confirmation of that diagnosis and then we'll note anything else we might find.'

'Yes, ma'am.'

'Alright—' she stood – 'let's get suited up, get into our party clothes, and . . . we'll see each other in there.'

Ten minutes later, Hennessey, having changed into green disposable paper coveralls, including green paper slippers encasing his feet and with his head encased in a matching hat held in place by an elasticated rim, stood reverently against the wall of the pathology laboratory. The room was illuminated by filament bulbs set in the ceiling behind Perspex screens which filtered the bulbs flickering. Four stainless steel tables stood in a row in the room, a bench containing small metal drawers ran along the length of the farther wall from where Hennessey stood. The floor was covered in industrial grade linoleum, shiny with disinfectant seal. Dr D'Acre also stood in the room as did Eric Filey the pathology laboratory assistant. Both of whom were smiling, also wearing similar green disposable coveralls. Hennessey had met Filey on numerous previous occasions and found that he liked the man. Warm and humorous, the portly young assistant had a freshness and a sanguinity noticeably lacking, in Hennessey's experience, in the majority of pathology laboratory assistants. But, in fairness, he reflected, observing and assisting in the dissection of corpses is not an occupation which encourages light-heartedness. On the table, furthest from the door, lay the corpse of Edwin Hoole, naked, save for a starched white towel placed over his genitals and which rode up against his expansive stomach. There was, in the room, an over-whelming smell of formaldehyde.

'The body—' Dr D'Acre adjusted the microphone that was attached to an angle poise arm, which in turn was bolted to the ceiling so that it was level and a few inches from her mouth – 'is that of a well-nourished, white European male, whose identity is confirmed as being that of Edwin Hoole, sixty-six years. The police are interested, the death already observed to have been suspicious, so the name can be added to the case number, Julie . . . something of nine zero two this year . . . three, I think.' She turned to Hennessey, 'Two post-mortems have been done already today. A bad smash on the Ring Road yesterday. My colleagues did the p. m.'s this morning while I was at the other side of the lab, on that table there at the end, looking at my friend's son, or at least his body.' She smiled. 'He had a tattoo I didn't know about and I doubt my friends knew about it either. It's been a long day and it's far from over yet.' She returned her attention to the body of Edwin Hoole. 'There is obvious major trauma to the head, swelling is apparent and extensive. No other injury to the body on the anterior aspect is evident.' She spoke, clearly so, for the benefit of a skilled and clearly well-thought-of audio typist, a very competent woman evidently called Julie who knew what and what not to type. Dr D'Acre reached for a scalpel from the instrument trolley beside the dissecting table and with a calm and practised hand she drew the blade of the scalpel round the circumference of the skull just above the ears. She placed the scalpel in the disinfectant-filled bowl beside the instrument trolley and then removed the scalp from the skull which detached with a sucking sound, clearly heard by Hennessey who stood in respectful silence some ten feet distant. She laid the scalp on a white cloth on the bench by the wall, which she then covered with a large tissue. Dr D'Acre then bent forward and commenced a close examination of the skull. 'And one to make sure . . .' she commented softly and then clearly for the benefit of Julie the audio typist, she said, 'Two linear fractures of the skull are noted, one at the side of the skull, just above the left ear and a second to the very crown of the skull. The first blow to be sustained being the one at the side of the skull.' She turned to Hennessey. 'Would you care to look at this, Chief Inspector?'

George Hennessey stepped forward, padding silently over the linoleum and stood beside Dr D'Acre. 'You see the clearly depressed fracture of the skull—' she indicated a clear depression to the left side of the skull – 'as you see, thin fractures from this blow cracked the skull in many directions and these radiate from the depression, not towards it as was once thought.'

'I see.'

'The second fracture here, at the top of the skull also caused hairline fractures to radiate from it, but where the fractures from this injury meet the fractures from the first blow they are stopped, or halted, and proceed no further.'

'Ah . . . I see.'

'We can tell from this that the blow to the side of the skull was the first to be sustained. In other words, the skull will crack until it meets a pre-existing fracture. So he was hit first at the side of the head and then as he slumped forwards, a second time on the top of his head.'

'Two to be sure, as you said.'

'Yes. Seems like it. The first blow would probably have been fatal.' Dr D'Acre looked at the man's face and then upturned his palms. 'Clean,' she observed, 'very clean.'

'Attacked indoors?' Hennessey glanced at her.

'Possibly, in fact that would be my guess. If he had been attacked out of doors I would have expected to see soil and grit, possibly traces of vegetation.'

'So, attacked indoors, left for dead, but he managed to get up and try to reach hospital.'

'A possibility.' Dr D'Acre patted the stomach of the deceased. 'Let's see what we have in here.'

Hennessey retreated to the wall and took a series of deep breaths. He noticed Dr D'Acre and Eric Filey similarly beginning to inhale and exhale deeply, and finally inhaling one last time before Dr D'Acre took a scalpel and drew it across the stomach until the gas within escaped with a loud 'hiss' and as it did so, Dr D'Acre and Eric Filey turned their heads to one side.

'Not as bad as some we have had, eh, Eric?' She smiled as she waved at the air in front of her.

'Indeed, ma'am.' Eric Filey smiled. 'In fact that was not bad at all.'

Dr D'Acre opened the incision and peered into the stomach. 'Well, he was hungry when he died, nothing in his stomach other than a little mulch . . . which is—' she picked up a little 'mulch' with the tip of the scalpel – 'peanuts,' she announced triumphantly, 'peanuts on an otherwise virtually empty stomach. He was in a pub just before he died, drinking and eating peanuts because he was feeling a little peckish. Just a guess but he hadn't ingested any food for six to eight hours before he was attacked, save for a bag of peanuts. His body is well nourished; he was used to three meals a day. So, let's turn to the mouth, always a goldmine of information.' Dr D'Acre opened the jaws with a stainless steel rod forcing them to give with a 'crack' as rigor was broken. 'Well, we have more peanuts in gaps between his teeth, but other than that he addressed the issue of dental hygiene. He cared for his teeth. Staining by mouthwash is evident . . . inevitable fillings but overall his dentist would be pleased with him. A good patient who kept his appointments, brushed regularly and rinsed with mouthwash. Right . . . back to the skull. Eric, can you pass me the saw, please.' Eric Filey handed Dr D'Acre a compact handheld electric saw with a circular blade. Dr D'Acre switched the saw on and the blade began to rotate at high speed, making a high-pitched whine as it did so, and which caused Hennessey to wince and grit his teeth. Dr D'Acre applied the saw to the side of the skull and drove it round the perimeter, following the line she had previously drawn with the scalpel to permit her to remove the scalp, thus separating the top of the skull from the remainder. 'Yes,' she said as she laid the fragmenting sector of the skull to one side, 'come and see Chief Inspector . . . subdural haematoma it is.'

Once again Hennessey walked silently across the floor of the pathology laboratory and stood beside Dr D'Acre.

'The human brain,' she said. 'Very healthy . . . some

shrinking might be in evidence at his age but there is none, so he enjoyed his faculties still, no mental degeneration but there the brain is a bright red colour, and here, at the points of the fractures it is darker.'

'Blood?'

'Blood. It's as good an example of subdural haematoma as you are likely to get in fact. Eric, can you get a close-up colour photograph of this please? I'll use it when I teach the medical students who have opted for the pathology course. Very infra dig but some are inspired to apply for the course.'

'Infra dig?'

'Oh, yes, we pathologists are third division doctors. The first division are the surgeons whose skill saves lives, second division is the family GP, first line of defence against any illness and we are third for all our patients are deceased by the time they reach us. Any pressure on us is to ensure we make a correct diagnosis as to the cause of death . . . a criminal trial might turn on it . . . but that is modest pressure compared to performing keyhole surgery.' She drummed her slender fingers on the side of the stainless steel table, 'But cause of death is confirmed, his brain tissue died where it came into contact with the blood.'

'That caused death?'

'Yes.'

'Why should it make his heart stop beating?'

'We don't know, a massive stroke has the same effect. The damage is to the brain, but the heart stops as well. Medicine is far from being a perfect science.' She paused. 'So that will be my findings. I confirm the casualty doctor's suspicion that this was a case of SDH following two blows to the head from a linear instrument . . . an iron bar for example, and as such, this is murder most foul. I'll trawl for poisons for forms' sake, of course. I may still be able to detect a trace of alcohol if he did spend the last evening of his life in a pub, but I doubt it will have any bearing on the case and I will fax my report to you a.s.a.p.'

*   *   *

'Thank you.' Vivienne Hoole held the phone against her ear using both hands, but applied only a gentle grip. 'Thank you, that's very kind of you. The Midnight Bell you say, at South Pidsey? Yes, I'll make arrangements to collect it. Thank you again, so kind of you to phone me.'

Charles and George Hennessey sat in the kitchen of Hennessey's home in Easingwold. George Hennessey glanced out of the window. 'Going to rain tonight.'

'Yes, I'll be on my way soon.'

'Yes.' George Hennessey curled his hands round the still warm mug of tea. 'He won't like it.' He nodded to the brown mongrel curled up in a wicker basket on a tartan rug beside the central heating radiator. 'He'll jump up and down with glee when I reach for the lead but when I open the door and he sees it's raining, he'll dig his heels in and I'll have to drag him out but out he has to go.'

'All dogs are like that. So, what's new?'

Hennessey told his son about the developing Edwin Hoole murder.

'You're right I think, just doesn't sound like a random attack. The earlier death of his brother that they thought suspicious, going out to meet someone, I think you are right to be suspicious.'

'We'll see how far we get . . . and you? Bradford you say?'

'Yes, defending a felon who definitely did not commit alleged offence despite compelling evidence to the contrary. Both myself and his solicitor have done all we can to persuade him to go G, because that way he'll get a lighter sentence, but he insists on going NG. I think he's probably convinced himself in his own mind that he really didn't do the crime and he won't be unconvinced.'

'Often the case. So, when do I see my grandchildren again? It's been a few weeks.'

'Yes, they're hankering after a visit to granddad's, hankering after being spoiled rotten.' Charles Hennessey grinned. 'And when are we going to meet your ladyfriend, that's more to the point?'

'Oh, soon, I think. She has indicated her wish to meet you and the grandchildren.'

'Good, so that is progress in the right direction. You know it's only now that I realize how hard it must have been for you to bring me up alone.'

'I had help.'

'Not the same as a partner.'

'No, but nobody could replace Jennifer. I am very, very fond of my ladyfriend but Jennifer . . . well . . .'

'Yes, I am sorry.'

'But the memories are golden. The holiday we had in Ireland after we were newly wed, not a honeymoon but as good as. Do you remember her?'

'Yes, I remember a figure, a person. I remember being in her lap and thinking that this person is important somehow. It's my first memory in fact and I was just three months old . . . and they still don't know what it is?'

'SDS.' Hennessey sipped his tea. 'Sudden Death Syndrome . . . just walking through Easingwold one hot Saturday, people thought she had fainted, that's how it appeared, but she was dead on arrival. Anyway, there could never be anyone else, until perhaps now. I've told her. You know I talk to her each day in the evening just looking out over the back garden where her ashes are scattered, telling her of my day and in the summer, I told her of my ladyfriend and I swear I felt wrapped around by a warmth which I couldn't explain. More than the sun, something . . . other worldly . . . glad I did that.'

'Told the garden?'

'Yes, and I am glad I built the garden according to her plan. Last thing she ever did, one of the last, before you were born. Sat at this very table designing the garden, right down to the pond at the bottom, it was just a flat expanse of lawn when we moved in, but you've seen the photographs.'

'Yes . . . and her plan . . . you framed it.'

'Yes, of course, I kept pretty well everything of hers except her clothes, they went to a charity shop in Leeds. Drove them out to Leeds one night and found a charity

shop there and left them in the doorway. I didn't want to
see some other woman wearing her coat.'

'Understandable, and sensible.'

Later, when his son had departed, George Hennessey
cooked a simple but wholesome supper and while it settled
he read an account of the Battle of Inkerman in 1854 during
the Crimean War. It was a recent acquisition to his collection of military history and he found it an enjoyable read
and enjoyed and appreciated the generous quality and the
good quality of the maps and diagrams in the book.

Later, as he anticipated, he took a protesting Oscar a rain-
soaked walk, out for half an hour to a field where the dog
usually criss-crossed with interest but on that occasion he
stood sulking at Hennessey's feet and so successfully forced
an earlier return home. Later still Hennessey strolled out
alone, wrapped up in a coat and fedora, to the Dove Inn in
Easingwold, for a pint of brown and mild, just one before
last orders were called.

It was Tuesday, 22.57 hours.

THREE

Wednesday, 10 February, 09.10 hours – 12.10 hours
*in which an inward-looking village is visited
and smoke begins to rise.*

George Hennessey glanced to his left and out of the small window of his office at the ancient walls of the city which, at that moment, glistened as the sun evaporated the frost which had formed on the stones during the previous night. The sky above and beyond the walls was, that morning, a vast area of unblemished blue, though the ground temperature was still just above freezing. He turned to his team, Yellich, Pharoah, Ventnor and Webster. 'Turned round alright, Ventnor?'

'Yes, sir, thank you—' DS Ventnor nodded – 'just needed a little sleep. I'm back into the daytime swing of things now.'

'Good man.' Hennessey smiled warmly. 'Well, we mustn't lose the impetus, have to keep the momentum going, but we also must not lose the overview. There were some developments while you were resting, Ventnor. Sergeant Yellich, perhaps you could . . .?'

'Yes, sir.' Yellich sat forward and gave what Hennessey felt to be an intelligent summary of the case to date; the confirmation of the identity of the deceased, the post-mortem findings, the mysterious sequence of phone calls, the private nature of the Hoole family which kept even their wives ignorant about certain matters, the belief held by the Hoole family that Harold Hoole's death some eighteen months previous had an air of suspicion about it and that Edwin Hoole was believed to have been meeting someone in connection with his brother's death on the day he was murdered.

'Thank you, Sergeant.' Hennessey patted the phone on his desk. 'One additional piece of information, Mrs Hoole phoned this morning, first thing, she told me that she had received a phone call from a pub, The Midnight Bell, which is in a village called South Pidsey. Confess, I have not heard of it but the pub landlord phoned her. Her husband had left his umbrella in the pub, left it there on the evening that he was attacked and murdered . . . a lead, no less.' He smiled broadly. 'So, let's go and talk to the landlord. So, what's for action?'

The team remained silent, but Hennessey saw that each officer was eager and alert. 'Suggestions?'

'Visit the pub as you say, sir, it sounds a promising lead. The p. m. told us he had been in a pub, the peanuts in the stomach, it ties in neatly.'

'You've just talked yourself into a job, Ventnor.' Hennessey grinned.

'Yes, sir.'

'Perhaps we ought to take a fresh look at the death of Harold Hoole, sir,' Carmen Pharoah suggested, 'an active man dying like that, as though he was a couch potato, sitting in front of daytime television which he allegedly loathed. I can see why the family are suspicious even if there was no sign of foul play, no evident sign anyway.'

'OK.' Hennessey continued to grin. 'You too have talked yourself into a job.'

'Yes, sir.'

'You know, sir,' Yellich offered, 'I'd be interested to know who bought Harry Hoole's house.'

'Oh—' Hennessey sat back in his chair, causing it to creak loudly – 'you would? Why? Is there some relevance there?'

'Well, sir, it would be coming at the issue of the sale from another angle. Was it suspiciously inexpensive, that sort of thing? Releasing the equity was clearly an issue for the family, especially when Mr Harold Hoole had two sons who would benefit from inheriting the property more than they would if they inherited what was left of whatever their father had sold it for.'

'Yes.' Hennessey nodded. 'A good point, a good point indeed.'

'I would think that Mrs de Vries, Edwin Hoole's first

wife might be a person to talk to,' Webster suggested, 'she was, I think, described as a 'cold fish' but cold or not, she was Mrs Edwin Hoole when her brother-in-law died in circumstances we are beginning also to feel are suspicious. She might be worth a visit.'

'Alright, leave no stone unturned, we'll do that; introduce ourselves to the lady, see if anything comes of it. So plenty to do, plenty to go on, you do that, Webster.'

'Yes, sir.'

'So, Sergeant Yellich, you team up with DC Webster. And DC Pharoah and DC Ventnor, you two team up.'

'Yes, sir.'

'I'll issue a press release about the murder of Edwin Hoole, it might provoke something. The commander wants me to be more office-bound these days, he's concerned for my health but I will be as hands on as I can. I will have another look at the road accident that claimed the life of Mrs Harry Hoole just a few months before he released the equity in his house, there might well be a connection. I'll also pick Dr D'Acre's brains about the death of Harry Hoole, the very non-couch-potato who died a couch potato's death. She may have an interesting comment or insight to offer.' He paused. 'Right, that's it, we all know what we are doing. Meet here tomorrow for a review unless a major development should develop.'

The first, and indeed the lasting impression that Detective Constables Pharoah and Ventnor had of The Midnight Bell pub was that one had to know it existed in order to go there. The village of South Pidsey revealed itself to be at best, thought Ventnor, uninspired and uninspiring; dull, rundown and at worst, he felt, it might be described as near a ghost town or a still living but lost village as can be had anywhere in rural England. The village was found by turning off the A1079 road near Bamby Moor into a narrow but inviting-looking lane which seemed to run endlessly between stands of thick woodland interspersed at infrequent intervals by meadowland. It was also a lonely road, no car was ahead of them, or behind them, or came towards them for the entire three miles that was the distance between the A1079 and South Pidsey. The village initially appeared deserted, no person was to be seen, the buildings appeared to be in a poor state of repair with peeling paintwork and tiles missing from roof tops, and the few motor vehicles that were parked at the side of the main road were sufficiently aged that they all seemed to belong to an earlier era, giving the impression that time had stood still in South Pidsey for the last twenty, even thirty years. It was all very still, all very silent, as Ventnor halted the car and on impulse wound down the window. Even birdsong was absent. The windows of the houses which lined the main street were intact and here and there a light shone from within and that was the only noticeable indication that the officers could see that told them that South Pidsey was inhabited.

'Strange place,' Ventnor commented.

Carmen Pharoah thought Ventnor's comment a little obvious, and needless, but she did have to concede that 'strange place' did indeed sum up their first impression of South Pidsey. 'No other Pidsey,' she observed as she glanced at the road atlas. 'No North, East or West Pidsey . . . no Great Pidsey, or anything at all, just South Pidsey.' She looked about her. 'Post Office,' she said, pointing to a red Royal Mail sign that protruded from a building about ten feet above the pavement and about one hundred yards from where Ventnor had halted the car.

Carmen Pharoah and Ventnor walked to the post office and entered and saw it clearly doubled as a grocery shop. As they pushed open the door a bell jingled and echoed loudly within the building. The interior of the post-office-cum-grocery-shop was gloomy and the eyes of the officers took a few seconds to focus. Eventually they identified a long counter on which stood a manually operated bacon slicing machine, at the side of which was a glass canopy beneath which were toiletries and sweets. Behind the standing space at the counter was a series of solid wooden shelves upon which were placed packets of cereals and washing powder. To the right of the counter, at ninety degrees to it was a brass grill, behind which was another counter: clearly the post office of South Pidsey. It took a further few seconds for Ventnor and Pharoah to realize that the dull shape behind the grill was a human being, who stood, absolutely still, eyeing the two strangers with owl-like curiosity and hawklike menace, and yet saying not a word. Carmen Pharoah saw the postmistress first and walked towards her. Ventnor followed as he too made out the figure camouflaged in the gloom, behind the grill.

'Good morning,' Carmen Pharoah said. 'We're looking for directions.'

The postmistress blinked once but otherwise made neither sound nor motion.

'We're looking for the Midnight Bell pub,' Carmen Pharoah pressed.

The woman breathed deeply as her eyes began to burn into Carmen Pharoah with undisguised hostility.

'We're police officers,' Ventnor growled, 'and we're hungry. We did not have a large breakfast.'

'What my colleague is saying,' Carmen Pharoah allowed menace to creep into her voice, 'is that you could be prosecuted for obstructing the police in the course of their enquiries, which, apart from anything else would be the end of your employment as postmistress, here or anywhere, Her Majesty's Post Office not approving of criminals behind its counters.'

Again the woman blinked and after holding the pause as long as she clearly felt safe to do so, she then inclined her head to her left and said, 'Left out of the door, and turn left at the end of the street. Can't go on anyway, South Pidsey is a dead end. You'll see the pub.'

The Midnight Bell was a small pub, so saw Pharoah and Ventor who had elected to walk there, being both needful of a little exercise and what fresh country air they could experience. The building was little more than the size of a substantial cottage, set against the road with a small beer garden to the left-hand side, in which were three wooden tables with built on benches, and which were presently covered with large waterproof sheets, as if mothballed

for the winter. The other side of the building was occupied
by the garden of the adjacent cottage, and the rear of the
building gave rapidly to woodland. If you drank at The
Midnight Bell, you walked there. The sign above the door
showed a church steeple against a dark background. Like
the paint on the houses of South Pidsey, the paint on the
pub's sign was faded and peeling and the sign itself creaked
as it swung in a sudden zephyr. The door of the pub was
solid, wooden, studded with black painted nails. Once
varnished, but now that too, like the paint, was faded and
peeling. In places patches of naked wood could be seen.
Ventnor stepped forward and knocked on the door. The
sound of the knocking carried around him but there was no
response from within. Ventnor glanced about him and saw
that, to his left, an elderly man had left his cottage and had
walked to the front gate of his property and stood, resting
on the gate, eyeing Ventnor and Pharoah in the same
distrusting, and raptor-like manner as had the postmistress.
Ventnor hammered on the door with the palm of his hand
and succeeded in obtaining a reaction in the form of a
window above him opening. A man in his thirties, straggly
haired, unshaven, and dressed in a Prussian blue dressing
gown, peered down at the officers, holding the window open
with one hand.

'Help you?' he asked, refreshingly cheerfully.

'Police.' Ventnor looked up at him, smiling in response
to the man's cheerfulness and thinking that he, at least, did
not seem to be of the manner of the residents of South
Pidsey.

'Police?'

'Yes.'

'Any trouble?'

'Plenty.' Ventnor grinned. 'There wouldn't be a police
force if there wasn't trouble, but right now we are just
looking for information.'

The man returned the grin but also couldn't conceal a
look of relief in his eyes. 'I'll be down in a jiffy.' He withdrew, closing the window behind him.

Ventnor read the inscribed plate over the doorway, dated

the previous year, which gave the licensee's name as being one Patrick Mutlaw. He looked about him. The old man still leaned on his gate still fixing the officers with a hostile stare. A lone rook cawed, the trees were rustled by a sudden breeze and the pub sign creaked as it was swung to and fro. There was, observed Ventnor, significantly more sound than movement in the village at that moment. Eventually the door of the pub opened, silently, swinging easily on evidently well-lubricated hinges and the man who had peered down at them, now looked up at them. Unusually, very unusually in both Ventnor and Pharoah's experience for any pub in the UK but especially unusual in the Vale of York which has a high water table, patrons stepped down from the street into The Midnight Bell.

'High ground,' the man said, noting the officers' surprise and realizing their observation. 'The village becomes an island when it floods round here, just a matter of about twenty feet, but it enables the houses to have cellars and for the pub floor to be below ground level, makes it very snug in winter and cool in summer. Do come in.' He turned and led the officers into the gloom of the pub. He was still dressed in his dressing gown and had pushed his feet into an old pair of trainers.

'You're Mr Mutlaw?' Ventnor asked, adjusting his eyes to the gloom.

'Aye . . . Pat Mutlaw at your service and everybody else's as well.'

Ventnor and Pharoah cast observant eyes around the room. An open fire built into the wall opposite the bar dominated the room with the remains of a coal fire in the grate. Kindling lay neatly stacked beside the ancient cast iron range. Equally ancient-looking wooden tables had ashtrays upon them of an inexpensive 1930s' bakelite design, each of which had been roughly swept of ash and cigarette butts but which still lacked a proper cleaning. The pub still smelled strongly of stale cigarette smoke.

'Can I get you some coffee?' Patrick Mutlaw asked, having reappeared behind the short wooden bar after disappearing into the gloom unnoticed by Ventnor and Pharoah as they read the room. He ran his fingers through his untidy mop of hair. 'I'm having one.'

Carmen Pharoah glanced at the ashtrays and smelled the stale cigarette smoke and said, 'Not for me, thank you.'

'Me neither,' Ventnor added, as he glanced at Pharoah and raised his eyebrows.

'Suit yourself.' Patrick Mutlaw retired from the bar, once again disappearing into the gloom and was then heard making instant coffee, filling a kettle, tapping a teaspoon against the rim of a mug. A few moments later he returned to the bar room and sat at a table nursing a cup of black coffee. He squeezed his eyes. 'Perks of the licensed retail trade—' he yawned – 'late mornings. Work late into the night but I can start each day with a warm bath. That's why I haven't dressed yet; I'll climb in for my morning soak when you've gone. That is if you don't arrest me.' He grinned and sipped the coffee and then groaned with satisfaction. 'The first caffeine of the day, it hits the spot, then the first fag and I'll be a very happy camper, but I'm getting better, don't light up my first fag until midday now, used to be the case that I'd grasp a fag as soon as I woke up. Do, please, sit down.'

'Good for you—' Carmen Pharoah laid a carefully manicured finger on the ashtray as she and Ventnor sat opposite Mutlaw – 'but this isn't strictly legal, not any more.'

'Nor is burning coal.' Ventnor inclined his head towards the range. 'Have difficulty moving into the twenty-first century do you?'

Pat Mutlaw shrugged. 'Well I don't, but South Pidsey does. It's a risk I take. The law never comes to the village unless there's trouble and then it has to be really big trouble. Most often the village sorts its own issues out. There's no other pub in the village and if I stopped the punters smoking I'd get the windows put in. It's the first thing I learned when I came here. It's not my pub; I just serve the drinks and take the money.' He glanced over the shoulders of the officers at the window, beside the door, and through which pale sunlight was entering. 'That was lesson numero uno.

I've been in the licensed retail trade for ten years, since I was eighteen serving behind the bar that was in the Merrie Monk. Know it?'

'Doesn't ring any bells,' Ventnor replied.

'Well it does a lot of trade with the university types, all the youngsters who are going somewhere, doing something with their lives. It began to eat at me, I was just treading water. Then two Christmases ago there was an incident, some colliers came in looking for booze and trouble and one of them got really familiar with the young girl who was working behind the bar and I . . . well, I just lost it and planted him one. He went down. The landlady cooled it off, smoothed things over. The police were not called and the collier boys left. Anyway me and the landlady talked it over the next day and I said I was angry about not going anywhere and she said I should have told her, told her I wanted to go further. Anyway, she had a word with the brewery and they said that they could use me at "The Bell", the present landlord there was itching to retire but nobody wanted it, so they helped me get my licence. The deal is that if I can turn "The Bell" round, as you say, sir, bring it into the twenty-first century, then I'll get an under-manager's post in a pub in York and then a paying pub of my own. That's the plan.'

'Could be a costly plan—' Ventnor raised his eyebrows – 'flouting the law like that, like this, it could cost you your licence.'

Mutlaw grimaced. 'Yes, I realize but it's more this village than it is me . . . it's not even in the twentieth century yet, never mind the twenty-first century and like I said, the police don't patrol the village, that and the island mentality, means that the villagers don't take to strangers or progress. I get a sort of cold acceptance being the beer fella, but that's all. I'm pleased I am by myself, no wife could cope with living like this.' He paused and sipped his coffee. 'That is my brief really, kick "The Bell" into the twenty-first century and do so without turning the village against me and the pub. If I can do that then the brewery can put a young husband and wife team in here and then I'll get an undermanager's post in a large pub in York and then a big one of my own.'

'Remove the ashtrays,' Pharoah suggested.

'Tried that, they just flicked the ash on the carpet or stubbed the fags out on the table tops and dropped the dog ends into the empty glasses, so I had to rinse each glass by hand before I could put them into the dishwasher. That was their way of protesting. I couldn't have been a tyrant because it's the patrons that really control the pub, any pub, not the landlord.'

'So I have heard,' said Ventnor nodding in agreement. 'I see your problem.'

'I also got an anonymous letter threatening to put bricks through the windows unless I returned the ashtrays and parts of this pub go back to the fifteenth century, so I value the windows and the frames that contain them.'

'Really?'

'Yes, it was largely rebuilt in the mid-nineteenth century but the cellar is very old and also the glass—' he nodded to the windows beside the door – 'that glass dates from the rebuild so it's now about one hundred and fifty years old and getting thicker at the bottom than the top, glass being liquid. So, I put the ashtrays back. I have the request not to smoke signs up, as you can see so I have made my position clear. The next step is to make the lounge—' he indicated behind him to deeper in the pub – 'I'm going to make that a non-smoking area. Announce it first, then try to enforce it a few weeks later. So I am addressing the issue, it's why the brewery gave me the pub.'

'We could help you,' Pharoah suggested, 'ask a uniform patrol to call. This village isn't a no-go area, there's no such thing.'

Mutlaw drew breath noisily between his teeth. 'Rather you didn't, that could go against me. You've got to keep these people onside.'

'They're flouting the law!'

'I know and I know I am party to that but they'll know that you have visited. You obtained directions from the post office didn't you?'

'Yes. How did you know?' Pharoah was genuinely curious.

'Because all visitors enquire at the post office and even if you didn't ID yourselves as police officers, Annie Kershaw the postmistress will have recognized you as being such and they might think I was asking for police assistance. They know my stance, they know of the smoking ban in public places and they're just dragging their feet to make a point of protest.'

'It's not something we can ignore, not for any length of time.'

'Appreciate that.' He drained his mug of coffee. 'Do you mind if I get another coffee? Sure you don't want a cup?'

'No . . . and sure,' Pharoah replied for both she and Ventnor.

Mutlaw returned a few moments later with a second steaming mug of black coffee. 'I need about three before I can function. As I said—' he slid back into his seat – 'frankly I have become accustomed to the slow and late start of a publican's day.'

'Soon be opening up for the day's trade.' Ventnor glanced at his watch, 'ten thirty now.'

Mutlaw grinned. 'I won't open until six p.m. no one wants any beer before then.'

'So when do you close?'

Mutlaw gave Ventnor a knowing smile. 'Well, it's rural England and like the vast majority of pubs, I will be operating a lock-in.'

'You take risks.'

'That's life, but it is a lock-in, no one enters after closing time . . . but I serve after closing time, and as I said, that's common practice in rural England. I let my fire start dying about midnight and most of the punters are gone by half past. So, you didn't come here to talk to me about observance of the smoking ban and licensing hours. How can I help you?'

'You can be of some assistance we hope.' Ventnor leaned forward and rested his elbows on the table surface. 'It's useful that this is a remote pub, probably very useful.'

'Oh?' Mutlaw blew gently on his coffee. 'How so?'

'It means that you'll know your customers, your regulars, and also spot a stranger.'

'Well, yes to both. I dare say that is true.'

'Good. Now yesterday you telephoned a lady called Mrs Hoole.'

'Oh, the umbrella? Yes, I have it behind the bar, didn't realize it was significant enough to merit two CID officers calling on me.' Mutlaw smiled at Ventnor.

'Unfortunately, it's probably very significant.' Carmen Pharoah spoke softly yet also coldly, annoyed that Mutlaw seemed to insist on speaking only to Ventnor, as if cold shouldering her for being black, or a woman, or both. 'Do you know the man who left it behind?'

'No.' Mutlaw shook his head. 'No, I don't, never seen him before, his name and phone number were on a label taped to the stem of the umbrella. Dare say he's a bit like me. I stopped buying umbrellas because I kept putting them down and forgetting them but he's more efficient than me, putting his name on it like that . . . but the number of umbrellas I have lost.'

'So who was the man?'

'A stranger, evidently called Hoole, but other than that a total stranger. They both were. I didn't know which of them was called Hoole. Why, anyway?'

'Because Mr Hoole, the owner of the umbrella was murdered shortly after leaving the pub. Very shortly after he left The Midnight Bell he was deceased.'

Mutlaw's jaw dropped. He sat back and rested against the bench on which he sat. It seemed to the officers to be a genuine reaction to the news, no feigning of shock, no overacting. 'Oh,' he groaned. 'God love us and save us . . . murdered, you say? Murdered in the sleepy Vale of York?'

'Yes, and it's not so sleepy, as our crime stats show,' Ventnor growled. 'So we are most keen to receive the utmost cooperation and we are both very sure that you will help us all you can.'

'Because,' added Pharoah icily, 'we can make things very difficult for you if you don't.'

'No need for threats . . . smoking in an out-of-the-way pub and late drinking, that's one thing but murder . . . that's quite another, a different kettle of fish.' He paused as if absorbing the significance of the police officers' visit. 'Of course I'll help all I can.'

'Good.' Ventnor smiled. 'So the two men, what can you tell us about them?'

'Well, both were strangers, both were of the same age group, middle-aged, both drank modestly, whisky and water, not beer. I recall them well, sat at that table, fully wiped clean now so you won't find their fingerprints on it but you're welcome to try.'

'Thanks, but as you say, it will be futile to try.'

'They were both posh.'

'Posh?'

'For this village they were posh, quite well dressed, and as I said, drinking whisky not pints of beer. Both seemed very intent on talking to each other, not just out for a drink to pass an evening, they had something to discuss that was plain but didn't want to be seen together. That was the impression I had, as if they came to "The Bell" because they knew no one they knew would be likely to also come here and notice them talking to each other.'

'I see.'

'I mean, you've seen the village, you have to know that the pub is here. You even have to know the village is here, it's on the map but there's only the one road. The road out there goes to a few houses then it peters out, becomes a track, then a footpath which leads to a field. One road into the village, same road back out. A couple of other roads lead off the centre of the village but they also just go to a dead end, one to a farm, the other to a row of cottages. So it really is one road in and the same road back out. South Pidsey really is a strange place . . . there's only one family.'

'Really?' Ventnor gasped.

'The Renshaws. There are family units with other surnames of course, but they're all related to the Renshaws in some way, some more distant than others but there is always a blood tie somewhere. The villagers even look similar. They don't gather on the village green and howl at the full moon but if they did do that I wouldn't be surprised.'

'Yes,' Ventnor agreed, 'I think we are beginning to get a feel of South Pidsey. Now, can you describe the man Mr Hoole was talking to?'

'I don't know which one was Mr Hoole. I just know that one of them left the umbrella.'

'Fair enough,' Ventnor conceded. 'Mr Hoole was wearing a sheepskin coat and cavalry twill trousers.'

'Oh, he sat with his back to the bar where I was serving so, of the two, I did get a better look at his companion.'

'Good.'

'I have them in my mind's eye, strangers, as I said, and so I took more notice. The other man was taller than Mr Hoole, thinner build; dark hair . . . let me remember.' Mutlaw closed his eyes. 'The other man wore a dark suit . . . blue I think, dark blue and he too had a winter coat which he took off. He sat nearer the fire, so he took his coat off. It was a long woollen overcoat. I thought the other guy had what you might call military bearing, again, just the impression I had . . . both were very eager to talk to each other.' Mutlaw stopped speaking suddenly and glanced to his left.

'You're remembering something,' Carmen Pharoah prompted.

'Yes—' Mutlaw put his hand to his forehead – 'he knew someone in here . . . who was it? As they were leaving he nodded to one of the villagers . . . who was it? Someone who sat at that table by the door. Who normally sits there?'

Thomson Ventnor and Carmen Pharoah remained silent.

'You know, I think it was Tom Thorpe. It was just a slight nod but Tom responded. Yes it was, it was Tom Thorpe, just nodded to him across the floor of the tap room.'

'They don't sound like tap room types,' Ventnor observed.

'Tap room or nothing midweek, just don't open the lounge, early evening, early in the week, no point, no one goes in there. The lounge is for weekend drinking, and there's no proper fire in the lounge anyway, not like the fire in here.'

'So where do we find Tom Thorpe?'

'Trying to think . . . I'm still new here you see . . . he's a regular, in every night . . .'

'We can't wait that long,' Ventnor said icily, 'dare say we could ask at the post office.'

'Oh, she'd love that, wouldn't she just love that.'

'I thought she might, so let's deny her that pleasure, shall we, keep her guessing.'

Mutlaw smiled. 'Oh, yes, let's. So, what can I tell you about Tom Thorpe? Tom is a sort of odd-job man, semi-retired. He has a state pension but it isn't enough to make ends meet if he wants his beer in the evening so he hires himself out but round folk's homes and gardens, not on the land. He's not fit enough for any hedging or ditching, that's hard labour, and that's not Tom Thorpe . . . but simple carpentry, filing down a door that's sticking, a bit of gardening in the summer, assembling a garden shed, that sort of thing.'

'Oh, we get the picture . . . we are still no nearer to finding him.' Carmen Pharoah allowed a serious tone to enter her voice. 'This is a murder enquiry, remember?'

'Well, I'd try Thorpe's Stores.'

'Sounds promising.'

'Can't miss it, it's in the village on the square, got all the stuff for sale outside on the pavement under a striped sun awning.'

'In this day and age?'

'South Pidsey,' Mutlaw shrugged. 'I told you, time drags its heels here. I think Tom might be related to the man who owns Thorpe's Stores. There are so few surnames in the village and, like I said, they're all related to the Renshaws. Sorry, it's the best I can do.'

Ventnor and Pharoah stepped up and out of The Midnight Bell and as they did so an elderly man lead a horse and cart along the road past the door, heading for the dead end of the road. The man passed without acknowledging them and the officers watched him in silence. Only the sound of

the horses' measured tread and the cartwheels crunching
the road surface told them that they were not looking at an
apparition.

'I fail to see how I can be of any help to you, really.' Ruth
de Vries was a small woman, finely boned with the classic
pinched face, straight-ahead stare, and complete absence
of humour of the criminal, so thought Webster and Yellich
likewise. Her lips were thin, her eyes focused to piercing
intensity and had no trace of emotional warmth. Her black
hair was closely cropped and she sat rigidly with an upright
posture in a wooden chair in the hallway of her house,
where she chose to receive her visitors. 'I am sorry to
hear about Edwin. Vivienne phoned me, but we are
divorced, not part of each other's lives any longer. I cannot
say that I am sorry; I mean about being divorced, it was
a good move. Sorry about Edwin, but not that we were
divorced.'

'I appreciate that—' Somerled Yellich spoke softly—'we
just need to find out as much as we can about him, we need
more background.'

'I see, but wasn't he a mugging victim or some such,
why the interest?'

'He may be,' Yellich replied cautiously, 'it is just too
early to say yet.'

'Oh.' Ruth de Vries looked up at Yellich. Tall, she thought,
even for a police officer, and he also seemed quite young
to hold Detective Sergeant rank. 'I would have thought that
the second Mrs Hoole would be the one to question, I know
little of his private life these days. Vivienne is the woman
to talk to.' Ruth de Vries sniffed at the name. She was stiffly
dressed in a calf-length skirt with matching blue jacket. Her
feet were encased in highly polished black boots with three-
inch heels. Her home smelled strongly of air freshener and
furniture polish. The hallway was wide, with high ceilings
in keeping with many other homes of the late nineteenth
century in Yellich's observation and experience. The chair
in which Ruth de Vries sat was one of a set of four, placed
two on each side of the hallway facing each other with a

set of drawers between two of the chairs and a highly polished table between the second pair. The maid who had opened the door to Yellich and Webster had walked away into the building to 'announce' the officers, and had then returned walking behind Ruth de Vries and introduced Yellich and Webster as, 'The police, ma'am'. She was thanked and dismissed by Ruth de Vries and shrank into the gloom of the interior of the building to be neither seen nor heard no more. Ruth de Vries sat down, without inviting Yellich or Webster to do the same and said that she failed to see how she could help them. 'I still think Vivienne is the person to ask,' she repeated.

'She is being questioned,' Webster replied icily.

'Your husband worked in the field of finance?' Yellich asked.

'Yes. The exact nature of which I never knew. We got divorced and I got pensioned off.' There was no attempt to hide the anger in her voice. 'The little woman no longer needed.'

'You seem to be very comfortable.' Yellich glanced at the hallway, 'This house . . . the maid.'

'And a gardener,' Ruth de Vries said abruptly. 'When I was divorced I did quite well but I still have to generate an income. But I have a head on my shoulders, I went into business.'

'Oh?'

'Property,' she said shortly, 'buying, developing, selling . . .'

'I see,' Yellich replied.

'Not alone. I have partners but I am not a kept woman. This—' she indicated her home – 'this is earned, bought and very nearly paid for. I have worked for it.'

'I see . . . so, your husband?'

'My ex . . . now my late ex . . . I did not remarry.'

'Yes, I apologize. So how long have you been divorced?'

'Ten years.'

'I see. What sort of man was your late ex-husband?'

'When I knew him he was very level-headed, feet solidly on the ground, a financier.'

'Shrewd?'

'Yes . . . yes—' she nodded, pursing her thin lips – 'yes, you could say that.'

'What about his brothers?'

'What about them?'

'How did they impress you, as people?'

'Harold and Leonard? Pretty much the same, all cast from the same mould as siblings are wont to be cast, both self-employed, Leonard with his garage, Harold who died recently, he had a chain of photographers requisites; shops, posh name for camera shops.'

'What was your ex-husband's attitude to inheritance?' Yellich asked the question suddenly.

Ruth de Vries eyes narrowed. She shot a cold glare at Yellich and then rapidly recovered her composure but the question had reached her, it had resonated with her, and both Yellich and Webster had noted it. 'Why?' she asked.

'It is,' Yellich replied, 'it is possibly, just possibly, of some significance.'

'How?'

'Just answer the question, please. What was his attitude to the issue of inheritance?'

'I assume he was in favour of it. We never discussed it. We were not planning for the end of his life when we were together, that really is a question for Vivienne, they will have talked about things like that, but he was a business man, he believed a man should provide for his own and leave his children something to give them a financial start in life. It's not really something we discussed, we didn't have children. We tried; it just didn't happen for us.'

'I see, and you had divorced by the time Harold died?'

'Yes . . . yes . . . I was . . . died of a stroke while watching TV and him so fit and healthy for his age. You see you can't escape it. And the way he used to sneer at folk who watched daytime television and what does he do but take a stroke while he's curled up on the sofa watching daytime television. There's rich for you.'

'You are Welsh?' Yellich asked suddenly.

'Originally. Why?'

'No reason, I just heard the trace of the accent just then in the Welsh phrase "for you" as in "there's tidy for you". I lived in Cardiff for a few years, just sufficient time to become acquainted with the accent and the turns of phrase like "by here" for "just here" and "for you".'

'I see. Well, there's observance for you.' She betrayed a brief smile. 'I am originally from Treorchy, just to the north of Cardiff but that's so long ago it seems like a different lifetime but yes, so there's observance for you.'

'Lovely accent.'

'Very similar to Hebridian.' Ruth de Vries seemed to become very keen to steer the conversation away from her late ex-husband and his family. Interesting, thought Yellich, very interesting. 'I used to get mistaken for a Hebridian person when I travelled in Scotland.'

'Really? Can't say I have been to the outer West of Scotland, so I'll take your word for it.'

'It is similar, the two accents are very similar.'

'We understand your sister-in-law was killed in a road accident?' Yellich pulled the interview back on track and noticed a look of dismay cross Ruth de Vries' eyes.

'Laura, you mean Laura Hoole, Harold's wife?'

'Yes.'

'Yes she was, that was a tragedy. I . . . we were divorced by then but we retained contact as ex's do, some more than others but yes, she was knocked down, a hit-and-run. I don't know any of the details but my nephew Keith, Laura's son; he's the one to ask. Their other son, Andrew lives away, in the south of England.'

'I see.'

'Keith has his own business now, metalwork. He started out by welding bits of metal to make garden braziers now he builds footbridges to go over new roads and things. He did well in a short time, very well.'

'Didn't inherit his parents' house though.'

'No, I believe not. Did inherit some cash but I don't know the details. He's in the Yellow Pages under Hoole Metal Fabrications. Andrew is also self-employed; he's in computers and mobile phones. It's the Hoole family ethos, self-help and enterprise, sort of "get up and go" spirit.'

'Any rivalry between the three Hoole brothers?'

'Yes, plenty of rivalry but no bad blood, no ne'er-do-well relative that caused shame on the family. Three brothers, Edwin, Leonard and Harold. Their father was a business man and they inherited his self-help attitude but of the three, only Harold had children.'

'I assume that there is no contact between yourself and Mr Leonard Hoole?'

'The sole surviving brother? No, no there isn't, we have no reason to be in contact with each other. There was little contact between me and my ex-husband, so even less with his brothers and I didn't need contact, I have done alright after the divorce. Look at my house, me and my partners did well in a few short years, buying property at the right time and selling at the right time. We never made a bad purchase, always cleared a significant profit on each transaction. You know, you two are in the wrong job,' she added with a knowing smile.

Louise D'Acre leaned back in her chair in her small, cramped office in the pathology department of York District Hospital. She closed the file and laid it on the working surface of her desk. 'I have to say,' she said quietly, 'I have to say that I would probably, nay certainly, yes certainly, have reached the selfsame conclusion, natural causes.' She avoided eye contact with DCI Hennessey. 'Not, and I dare say that is the crucial point, not because there is evidence of death by natural causes, there isn't. It would be because there is a complete absence of anything even suggestive of unnatural causes. Nothing suspicious leaps out at one when reading the report, and Colin Wheelhouse is a damn good pathologist. He is internationally renowned, internationally consulted and is the author of a seminal textbook and this department is lucky to have him.'

'I see.'

'You sound disappointed, Mr Hennessey.' Louise D'Acre

smiled briefly at him and allowed herself an equally brief
moment of eye contact.

'No . . . no—' Hennessey shrugged his left shoulder –
'not disappointed. It doesn't clear things up as I hoped it
might . . . still could be . . . still couldn't be, nothing hard
and fast either way.'

Louise D'Acre brushed the slender fingers of her right
hand through her short hair. 'Well, it's so easy to kill
someone without making it look like murder most foul. Did
he fall or was he pushed? Being the most obvious example,
but if you hold someone under water for long enough
without leaving any bruising or grip marks or other marks
of restraint, any pathologist would have to record a finding
of accidental death by drowning, despite it being murder.'
She picked up the file and reopened it. 'The one thing that
might just might indicate something of a suspicious nature
is the petechial haemorrhaging which Colin notes, little
pinpricks of blood spots in the eyes. That is common in
suffocation or strangulation or asphyxiation even but it also
occurs naturally, sometimes in the instances of brain
haemorrhaging.'

'A stroke?'

'Yes, so petechial haemorrhaging is not an indication of
suspicious circumstances, not in itself. Bruising round the
neck and petechial haemorrhaging, then yes, that is definitely
suspicious but such is absent in this case.'

'But little red spots in the whites of the eyes, by themselves, is not suspicious?'

'That's it. So Colin was being cautious. We must not
stick our necks out. "Seldom say never . . . seldom say
always", that's the rule.'

'So, if I was to press you . . .?'

'Oh, you mustn't.' Again a brief smile, but with an air
of admonition about it, and which was accompanied by
stern eye contact. 'You must not press me. Any pathologist
can only comment upon what he or she finds, science being
the study of observed fact.'

'Science is the study of observed fact,' Hennessey repeated.
'I like that. It's very clever, no guesswork, no interpretation

of possibilities, just the study of observed fact. Good enough.
So, can you comment on the likelihood of Mr Hoole being
a stroke victim?'

Yet again Dr D'Acre allowed herself a brief, very brief
smile. 'You're like a dog with a bone, Chief Inspector, you
just won't let go, will you?'

'Same issue, different angle of approach, has been useful
before.'

'Very well, the answer is again, I can't. Strokes can happen
to anyone at anytime; young, old, healthy, unwell, fit, out of
condition. Human or animal, if you have a brain and a circulation of blood, you can have a stroke. His medical notes
indicated that he did have high blood pressure but that was
being controlled by medication, so we can't read anything
into that. I can't say that he was a stroke waiting to happen.'
She read the file. 'The arteries were not dangerously clogged;
his heart was in excellent condition. The heart is a muscle,
the more you exercise it, the stronger it gets. A good, brisk
twenty-minute walk each day will keep a middle-aged man's
heart healthy and I understand Mr Hoole did more than that.
According to these notes he was a "grey jogger". He wasn't
at all overweight, he had no trace of alcohol or any form of
drug in his blood stream, so . . . in that sense he was a little
unlikely to be a stroke victim, but again, he was fifty plus,
he was in Indian Territory when it comes to strokes. He
wasn't in danger of having to circle his wagons but Indian
Territory is still Indian Territory . . .'

'As you say, fifty plus with a brain and a blood stream.'
Hennessey sighed.

'Death comes to anyone at any age, sometimes without
warning.' She paused and sank back into her chair and put
her hands to her forehead. 'I'm sorry, I didn't think.'

'It's alright,' Hennessey smiled. 'Anyway she didn't die
of a stroke which is what we are talking about.'

'Yes, but still, I am sorry.'

Hennessey glanced round the office, photographs on
the wall showed Louise D'Acre, her children and Samson
her stallion. 'What could induce a stroke, speaking
hypothetically?'

'Speaking hypothetically and I emphasize hypothetically, a plastic bag will do nicely, that would suffocate the victim and cause petechial haemorrhaging. But this was a stroke. Blood vessels had burst in his brain, that is a stroke, blood had come into contact with brain tissue and had destroyed the brain tissue, massively so, sufficiently so to cause death.'

'Could that be induced?'

'It could, but not in a predictable way. It is pretty well impossible to murder someone and make it look like a stroke, but a plastic bag over the head of someone who is conscious, as opposed to comatose, or sleeping, then that would cause panic and stress and if he had high blood pressure already, then yes, that could, in theory, induce a stroke. If that happened then the perpetrator had had a lucky day, especially since he had the presence of mind to take the plastic bag away with him. If that did indeed happen, by accident, he created what was fairly and reasonably diagnosed as death by natural causes . . . could have . . . could have.'

'Chances in ten?'

'Low . . . two or three chances in ten. No . . . no . . . I'd put it lower than that. You are drawing me, Chief Inspector.'

'I know, ma'am, it's like drawing teeth.'

'I do not appreciate you trying to do that,' she replied coldly, 'but a low chance, perhaps one in thirty, that sort of figure.'

'So, a very lucky murderer.'

'Very lucky if that did happen. Much, much more likely is that it was a stroke suffered by a man who had high blood pressure and was in his middle years of life and as such a sudden but natural death.'

'Tom Thorpe?' The man eyed Ventnor and Carmen Pharoah. 'Aye, I know him, I know Tom.' Silence. The man clearly wasn't going to give anything away.

'How do you know him?' Ventnor pressed.

'Family,' the man grunted. He was slightly built and wore a brown smock and stood in the midst of the floor of his shop surrounded by items for sale: paint brushes, metal polish, gardening tools, nuts and bolts, work wear. 'Hardware in a word', thought Ventnor, and the pleasantly 'new' smell that hung in the air reminded Carmen Pharoah of a similar shop near her grandmother's house on St Kitts. In an instant she was briefly, very briefly, transported home. Smell, she had always found, has an immediacy about it that the other human senses do not possess.

'Meaning?' Again Ventnor pressed the man for an answer.

'Cousin.'

'So where can we find your cousin, Tom Thorpe?'

'He's not in any trouble,' Carmen Pharoah offered with a ready smile and a look of warmth across her eyes.

'Not at all,' Ventnor assured the man. 'No trouble at all, we do need information that he might be able to provide. We think he can put us in touch with someone who is also not in trouble, but whom we desperately need to speak to.'

'That's all?'

'That's all, I assure you.'

'It's just that our Tom, he's done a few stupid things in his life when he was young and a bit in the drink but he's turned the corner, he's well turned it. Hasn't been in trouble with the law for a good few years now. I just don't want it all to start again.'

'Good for Tom, and like we said, we only want him to help us find someone.'

'It's difficult for him to trust cops at times and this village doesn't care for outsiders.'

'So we are learning,' Carmen Pharoah replied, dryly.

'I'll go and get him for you.'

'He's here?' Ventor asked, a little surprised.

The man nodded, indicating the area behind him. 'He's in the back. He works for me sometimes.' The man turned and walked away and disappeared, as if swallowed by the gloom of his shop's interior, just as earlier that day Pat Mutlaw had walked away from Ventnor and Pharoah to be swallowed by the gloom within The Midnight Bell.

When Tom Thorpe presented himself, somewhat sheepishly the officers thought, he was observed to be dressed in blue overalls and was wiping oil from his hands with a dirty cloth. Ventnor thought Tom Thorpe and his cousin, the proprietor of the shop, looked to be so similar that they could be mistaken for twins; the degree of inbreeding in the village of South Pidsey was becoming self-evident to the officers.

'Tom Thorpe?' Ventnor asked in a non-threatening manner.

'Aye.' There was an edge to his voice, a curiosity, a caution, a suspicion. 'Elliot said you said I haven't got to worry about anything, is that right?'

'Nothing from us, Tom,' Ventnor smiled. 'We were told you might be of help to us.'

'Oh?' His eyes were cold, steel-like; there was no depth in them that the officers could detect.

'Yes. You were in The Midnight Bell a few nights ago?'

'That's true because I am in there every night, a few jars, a game of dominoes or darts, both some nights, each evening from six until eight, sometimes nine. What else is there to do in this village in the evening but go to the pub? So yes, I was in "The Bell". I have no family so I work each day until pub time, then walk home and get up again the next morning. Each day is pretty much, as the day before it, the same for me.'

'So, two nights ago, you'll remember because there were two strangers in the pub that night . . . two men . . . sat at the table to the left of the fire drinking whisky, middle-aged, well dressed . . .'

'Yes—' Tom Thorpe nodded and appeared relieved – 'the two strangers.'

'One of the strangers was taller than the other, dark hair, suit. On the way out when they were leaving he was seen to smile at you. He recognized you.'

'Yes.'

'Who was that man? We really need to talk to him.'

'Is that all you want?' Tom Thorpe's relief was obvious. Despite what his cousin had said, it was clear to the officers that Thorpe hadn't fully turned the corner, he still had something to hide; he still had a reason to fear the police.

'That's all we want.'

'The man you want to speak to is called Woodgate, Mr
Julian Woodgate. He's a bit posh, I really was surprised
to see him in "The Bell". I shouldn't have brought him
there, shouldn't have done that. I got a hard time from
the boys in the village for bringing a stranger to the pub.
You bring one, then more follow, they said, and they were
right because Mr Woodgate brought that other guy in and
occupied a table that four regulars usually occupy so they
sat at someone else's place and that caused a bit of bad
feeling. It wasn't their pub and they sat by the fire where
Big Andy and Phil sit and their mob, that's where they
do the crossword puzzle, passing it about, one clue each
until it's done. Anyway, when they'd gone, Woodgate and
the other guy, the boys laid into me, verbally, I mean.
That's what happens when you bring a stranger in, they
said, it stops being the village pub and starts being a cosy
little pub for townies to drive out to, ruins it. And I felt
bad so I had to go home early that night before I'd had
my proper fill of beer and I didn't sleep well. It was my
way of saying sorry to the boys.'

'How do you know Mr Woodgate?'

'Did some work for him once, not long back.'

'Oh?'

'Yes, I built a fence round his garden. Before he set me
on he asked me if I had done any similar work, so I said
I had, here in South Pidsey and if he'd come, I'd show him
it and he did so. He drove out here and I showed him the
fence I'd put round a cottage in the village and he knocked
on the door of the cottage and the owner, Mrs Thorpe, but
not our branch of the family, she confirmed that I had built
it. So he was keen, asked if there was anywhere we could
go and talk terms. Well, it was early evening by then and
"The Bell" had opened and so we walked there and we
agreed the price and he seemed to take a shine to the pub
and remarked that it was "an out-of-the-way place", or words
to that effect, words like "you'd never stumble across it",
"you'd have to know it exists". You know words like that.
I knew then it had been a mistake to bring him to "The
Bell". Anyway, I did the job and he paid. Big job, nice bit

of work, dug a shallow trench round his garden; put the fence posts in, good coat of creosote. Lovely job on a summer day that, applying creosote and I like to work alone, I don't work well in a team. I wanted to be a postman for that reason, walking about all day, just me, my thoughts, and doing a useful job as well but I had a record for theft and so that was it. I do odd jobs now or help out here when Elliot needs a hand, servicing lawnmowers at the moment, getting them ready for spring.'

'So you'll know where Julian Woodgate lives?'

'It was my first case as a Detective Constable.' Street sat back in his chair. 'I remember it well. I can let you have a look at the file, of course, but you haven't driven out from York to read a file. I assume you want to visit the location?'

'Strangely, I don't think it's necessary—' Hennessey fed the rim of his fedora, damp from the rain, through his finger-tips – 'it's just nice to get out of the office. My boss has me deskbound these days, he's worried about my health. Good of him really, but I do like to get out of the office.'

'I see ... well the Hoole hit-and-run—' Street was a thin-faced man, his office window at Malton Police Station looked out over the red tiled rooftops to the rich farming country beyond, under a mantle of low, grey cloud – 'definitely murder, but it came to naught from our point of view.'

'Premeditated?'

'No—' Street shook his head – 'no, I ... we, didn't think so, we didn't form that impression. It seemed to us to be opportunist rather than premeditated. Mr Hoole was a busi-nessman, had a string of camera shops, as I recall, didn't appear to have enemies ... competition perhaps but no enemies and no enemies in his private life so far as we could tell.'

'I see.'

'So, one night he and Mrs Hoole were walking home, they had walked into the village where they lived and were walking along a straight section of the road home, which invites speed. It's about a mile long at that point, dimly lit, a low grass verge and a series of old-fashioned wooden fence posts.'

'Wooden?' Hennessey queried, genuinely surprised.

'Yes, not the concrete ones we have now, the council hadn't got round to replacing them with concrete ones. It took the Hoole accident to jolt them into action over that.'

'So, little protection from a car leaving the road?'

'None . . . and they, the fence posts, were very widely spaced as well. The council later put four concrete posts in for every one wooden post it removed. The council also built up a footpath so that it's now three feet above the road surface, then when the incident took place, the path and the road were virtually level with each other and there is a path only on one side of the road, so that when the Hooles were walking home the traffic was coming up behind them.'

'Understood.'

'It was apparently all over in a flash, in an instant, as it is sometimes the way of it. No warning at all. Unusually, she was on the outside, unusually in both senses, unusually that most couples walk with the man on the outside and unusually for them in that they normally did walk with Mr Hoole on the outside but that evening, for no reason at all, or for some reason we never found out about, he was on the inside and a car travelling at speed mounted the low verge, hit her and missed him, crashed into a wooden post which had probably been put in place before the Second World War, splintered it like a matchstick and drove on . . . all over in a second or two. All Mr Hoole could say was that it was large and dark in colour. One minute he was walking home with his wife after a pleasant and relaxing evening in the pub and the next he was a widower.'

'Yes,' was all Hennessey said, but Street's words reached him deeply.

'She was killed outright. The ambulance hurried her to hospital but she was declared DOA, as it was termed in those days. He was untouched, badly shaken, but totally unscathed. We had no leads, none at all. We alerted the garages in the locality, asking them to notify us if someone brought a large, dark-coloured car to them to have accident damage to the front repaired, but none of them did. We told them why we wanted information – a fatal hit-and-run – that annoyed the garage proprietors. I mean the crime annoyed them, not what we told them.'

'Yes . . . yes.'

'So they were motivated to help, but despite that, no result at all. So the trail went cold and went cold rapidly. It seemed that it was an opportunist crime, a motorist travelling at speed, no other cars about, probably angry about something in his personal life and, lo and behold, what was presented to him but a victim, maybe even two victims and no witnesses, the temptation was just too great. A very cowardly thing to do, but it happens.'

'Oh, I know. Or just a drunken driver who fled the scene.'

'Of course, sorry, sir. I was saying that more to myself than anything else.' Street paused and glanced out of his office window to the ploughed fields and denuded trees, to the skyline beyond. 'So, no motive, no leads, no damaged car. Days went, weeks, other crimes were committed. Limited resources had to be put to the best possible use and the incident became a "cold case".'

'How did Mr Hoole strike you? What was your impression of him?'

'I thought him a genuine personality. The grieving widower . . . lost, staring into space, seeming not to know where he was. He seemed to be quite dependent on his wife, emotionally speaking, which I thought strange for a businessman – they always strike me as being a hardbitten breed of men. He died a few years later, natural causes, I believe.'

'Yes,' Hennessey replied. 'Anything strike you as odd there?'

Street looked puzzled. 'No, we didn't think so. Sitting alone at home, we understand, and he had a stroke, nothing to interest the police. Why, did we miss something?'

'We don't know yet.'

'Yet?' Street's brow furrowed. 'I confess I'll be angry and upset with myself if we did miss something.'

'You needn't be. It is that something has come to light

which merits the police taking another look at Mr Hoole's death being that a few days ago, Mr Harold Hoole's brother Edwin died in suspicious circumstances, he was murdered.'

'I see.' Street clasped his hands together and rested them on his desk top. 'That is interesting.'

'Yes. He was attacked and probably left for dead, but managed to try to save his own life by staggering towards the hospital but hadn't got the legs.'

'Tragic.'

'Yes. But what makes it suspicious, is that he was believed to be meeting someone who had information about his brother's death. It didn't ring true to the family that the brother had had a stroke; he was very fit and active. Clearly he had recovered from his wife's death of some years earlier and he was particularly critical of folk who watch daytime television, yet he was found lying on the sofa in front of a flickering TV screen in the middle of the afternoon.'

'I see, but still insufficient to say foul play.'

'Don't be on the defensive, Mr Street.' Hennessey grinned. 'Nothing to reproach yourself for but frankly, I think smoke is beginning to rise.'

'Smoke, sir?'

'As in "where there is smoke, there is fire".'

'Oh?' Street sat forward.

'I spoke to the Home Office pathologist who looked at the notes of Mr Harold Hoole's post-mortem and she said, strictly off the record, that he could have been murdered.'

'Murdered?'

'Petechial haemorrhaging, little red dots in the eyes, can occur naturally as a symptom of a stroke, but can also occur when someone is asphyxiated.'

'Oh . . . smoke, as you say. Is there anything we can do to help?'

'Yes, I think I would like to visit the scene of the accident after all, I'd like to visualize it.'

'Of course, though the pathway has been built-up, as I said it's no longer at road level and the wooden posts have been replaced by concrete but yes, of course.'

'And if you could recommend a place to eat in Malton?'

'The George and Dragon,' said Street smiling, 'the Suffolk hotpot is of passing excellence. I eat there myself from time to time.'

'Well perhaps you'll join me?'

'I'd love to.' Street stood.

'Right.' Hennessey also stood. 'Site visit, then lunch.'

It was Wednesday, 12.10 hours.

FOUR

Wednesday, 10 February, 13.25 hours – Thursday, 11 February, 01.15 hours.
in which is learned of a woman and her pet, and Carmen Pharoah and Thomson Ventnor are severally at home to the gracious reader.

Carmen Pharoah and Thomson Ventnor did indeed find Julian Woodgate esquire to be 'a bit posh', as he had been described to them by Thomas Thorpe. They also found him to be a not particularly pleasant individual. He sat in a deep and high-backed armchair by a large fireplace in which a small fire was burning as if contentedly. He was dressed in a green-based, paisley-patterned, padded smoking jacket, pulling leisurely on a black cigarette that he had pushed into the end of an equally black cigarette holder. He seemed to be large-boned, well built, with a round, clean-shaven face, fleshy hands and a protruding stomach. Carmen Pharoah thought him the sort of man who could lie on the floor and still be able to look down his nose at another person.

'Yes . . . Thorpe, efficient little man, he did his job. I paid him minimal wage, of course.' Woodgate spoke softly.

'Of course,' Ventnor echoed dryly.

'Doing my bit. It's paying the minimum wage that helps the economy flourish and leads to a consumer boom and foreign investment. Why do you think it is the case that everything you buy these days seems to be made by Chinamen?' Woodgate flicked the ash from his Black Russian into a large ashtray that rested on the arm of his chair. 'Eh? Answer that. I'll tell you why, it's because they pay peanuts to their workers so they can sell their product, whatever it is, for peanuts. It's cheap and it works alright, so people buy it rather than buying British. We have to compete with them, that's the way I see it. So I paid Thorpe the minimum wage. He built a fence around my property. I supplied the wood and the weather-proofing . . . and . . . and—' he raised a finger – 'I also fed him. I did that. I told cook to prepare a midday meal for him each day that he was here. He probably spun the job out since he was being paid by the hour and he got a free lunch every day, but I budgeted for that because that's what he would have done.'

'Who would have done that?' Ventnor asked, sitting beside Pharoah on a wide and high-backed settee which matched the chair in which Julian Woodgate sat.

'He—' Woodgate jabbed the cigarette holder towards an oil painting which hung on the wall above the fireplace – 'he being Jacob Woodgate, my great-grandfather. He built this house and bought the grounds, forty-seven acres of the stuff. He'd be the sort of fella to spin a job out while it was paying.' Woodgate paused. 'Paper.'

'Paper?'

'Paper.'

'I don't follow,' Ventnor appealed.

'Neither do I,' Carmen Pharoah added, feeling a growing annoyance towards Woodgate.

'Paper—' Woodgate curled his finger over the top of the cigarette holder, and grinned, displaying a row of white teeth as he did so – 'paper, that's the family business. Ever heard of Woodgate Paper Limited?'

'Can't say I have,' Ventnor conceded.

Carmen Pharoah shook her head.

'That's because it doesn't exist.' Woodgate laughed at his own joke. 'Jacob was ahead of his time in that respect, at least in that respect, at a time in an age when folk were still naming business organizations after themselves or their partners. You know the model, Harland and Wolf for ship-building, de Havilland for aircraft.'

'Yes . . . yes.'

'Well Jacob thought that such would be a barrier to marketing and so he, at the cusp of the nineteenth and twentieth centuries, between the death of Queen Victoria and the outbreak of the Kaiser War, he founded YPI.'

'Ah, Yorkshire Paper Industries.'

'Yes, but it is a common mistake that people make to think that the "I" stands for "Industry" or "Industries". In fact it stands for "Interests" and he didn't get involved in the consumer product. Sold paper in a semi-finished form to other companies to turn into the product they sold to the consumer. We sold tissue for use in the bathroom, but not in the finished form, and paper pulped from timber growing in Canada, and also we obtain paper from recycled newspapers, we do our bit to save the planet. We even produce paper from cloth, the highest quality paper you can obtain. We sell that to Governments around the world for use for official records. It doesn't deteriorate if it's kept at minus one degree Celsius. Delicate stuff, paper, if you wish to preserve it, it has to be kept at a permanent minus one degree C, but anyway, I thought Tom Thorpe would spin out the job and so I budgeted for that. Should have agreed a fixed price rather than an hourly rate but he finished in a reasonable time and did a good job. So what's he done that is of interest to you? Confess I thought he looked a bit shifty, but I still have the family silver, so all's well.'

'He's not our area of interest,' Carmen Pharoah replied, coldly, fighting back an urge to growl at Woodgate.

'Oh?' Woodgate glanced sideways at her, sneering almost, she thought, as if believing that the presence of a police officer who was both female and Afro-Caribbean was gravely offensive.

'No,' Ventnor added, 'we are interested in yourself, sir.'

'Me?' Woodgate smiled. 'I am honoured, but do I need a lawyer?'

'Don't know, Mr Woodgate—' Ventnor continued to speak coldly – 'do you?'

Woodgate scowled at Ventnor, his affable manner evaporated in an instant. He glared at Ventnor. 'I do not care for jokes. Do not play games with me. Please.'

'No games,' Carmen Pharoah assured him. 'We are very serious. The man you had a drink with in The Midnight Bell in South Pidsey the other night, Edwin Hoole . . .'

'Yes?' Woodgate continued to scowl.

'He was murdered that same night.'

Colour drained from Woodgate's face. 'Well, I'll be blowed.' He took the cigarette holder from his mouth as a cloud of smoke rose lazily and dissipated about his head. 'Well, that is a turn up for the books. Murdered you say?' He glanced up and out of the twelve-foot-high windows of the drawing room in which he and the officers sat, out towards the forty-seven acres of grounds, containing lakes and stands of trees and walkways between shrubberies.

Carmen Pharoah and Ventnor both thought his reaction to the news of Edwin Hoole's murder to be genuine. They remained silent for a few moments and a silence descended within the room during which Carmen Pharoah glanced round the room, the oil paintings, the high ceilings, the velvet curtains, the Axminster carpet, and pondered upon the global market for paper, something she had not thought of before and conceded that it must be vast. It was then that a magnificent house in forty-seven acres of grounds made sense. It made all the sense in the world.

'Well—' Julian Woodgate glanced at Ventnor, pointedly ignoring Carmen Pharoah – 'now I understand your reason for visiting me. Murdered, well, I'll be damned. Nice fella, sort of local boy made good, but a nice fella just the same. Earnest, serious-minded but I'd prefer that to the comedian type.'

'You didn't know him before that night?'

'No.' Woodgate shook his head. 'Not my type really, you know, but pleasant enough, harmless sort.'

'But you went for a beer with him?'

'Went for a whisky with him, but yes, we had a drink, it was his suggestion. He wanted to meet in an out-of-the-way place. He didn't know one but didn't want to travel too far from York and so I said that I knew of the very place. So we went to The Midnight Bell in my car. It was suitably out of the way for him. In fact he said he thought it an ideal pub for the purpose. We arranged to meet just south of York and then I drove us both to the pub. It was just the place to come for a clandestine meeting. The locals didn't like it very much but they couldn't do a thing about it. Frankly I thought we would have been better staying in the car but he wanted a drink. He seemed a little nervous about something, like he was looking over his shoulder all the time. Murdered? So perhaps he had reason to be nervous, reason to be looking over his shoulder.'

'What did he want to talk to you about?' Ventnor asked.

'My sister. My older and late sister.'

'Late?' Carmen Pharoah echoed.

Woodgate glanced briefly in her direction and nodded. 'Yes, late. Sadly. Some people go before their time and Charlotte was one.'

'I am sorry,' Ventnor said softly.

'Yes.' Woodgate looked downcast. 'Yes, she was driving home; she was run off the road. It happened about twelve months ago. We were not very close, she was fully fifteen years older than me and had left the family circle, she was a bit errant, a bit wayward. She lived relatively close but we didn't see each other very often, a card at Christmas and that was it, but we knew where each other was and that was the main thing.'

'I see.'

'But her death was suspicious?' Carmen Pharoah clarified.

'Yes, suspicious but without apparent motive, no one benefited from her death, she had no enemies that were known of.'

'What happened?'

'Some joyrider in a large, fast car approaching her at night on a long, straight road suddenly veered in front of her. She was in a smaller, lighter car and she swerved. She wasn't wearing a seatbelt and was travelling at speed—' he opened up both his palms in a gesture of helplessness – 'she hated being confined by them, so it was her practice to drive without wearing it, especially at night when the police couldn't see she wasn't wearing one. She made no secret of it. She argued that she had the right to put her own life at risk if she chose to do so. Charlotte was very pig-headed, very stubborn . . . even as a little girl she was like that. Dare say you know the type?' He smiled at Ventnor and persisted in ignoring Carmen Pharoah. 'I used to feel sorry for her husband.'

'Used to feel sorry?'

'Yes, he predeceased her. He died of a heart attack, mid-sixties, a bit young but not tragically so, dare say it *was* his time.'

'Was she alone in the car?'

'Yes. It happened that a cyclist saw the whole thing, otherwise we would not have known why Charlotte's car had left the road. There was no collision, no skid marks, nothing. Her car left the road and hit a tree at speed, some joy rider probably getting his kicks by forcing another motorist off the road. We had no information in respect of the make of car, just that it was large and dark in colour. The cyclist in question was an old boy with failing eyesight and was an "every car looks the same to me" sort of moron. He could tell a big car from a small one and a light-coloured car from a dark-coloured one and that was about it. Oh . . . and a fast one from a slow one. He could tell those apart as well, hardly a star witness, but he told us enough to let us know why Charlotte's car left the road. It could make me angry if I let it.'

'It would make me very angry,' Ventnor replied coldly, 'and I would let it do so.'

Julian Woodgate twisted the stub of the cigarette from the holder and extinguished it in the ashtray. 'Well, I can understand that, I can well understand it but throughout my life I have tried to get angry about things I can do something about and only those things. Anger is such a destructive emotion; you have to use it if you are going to harbour it, that's the way I look at it. Believe me, if I knew the identity of the other driver, I would be angry and doing something about bringing him to justice, but I don't see the point of sitting here fuming about something I can't address.'

Ventnor doubted that he could muster such detachment in similar circumstances, but asked, 'So, tell us, why was Edwin Hoole interested in your sister's death?'

'He wasn't—' Woodgate smiled and took another Black

Russian from the packet and pushed it, lovingly almost, thought Carmen Pharoah, into the cigarette holder, whilst holding the pause in the conversation – 'it was her property that he was interested in, or rather her attitude to said property.'

'Oh?'

'Yes. She had released equity in her house some years earlier, she must have needed the cash.' Ventnor and Pharoah glanced at each other.

'Why?' Woodgate lit the cigarette with a chunky gold-plated cigarette lighter. 'Is that of some significance? I mean, you two looked at each other when I mentioned that she had released her equity.'

'It could be,' Ventnor replied.

'In fact it is.' Pharoah leaned forward and rested her elbows on her knees.

'That's what Edwin Hoole said.' Woodgate sat back in the armchair. 'He did say that his brother had done the same and that he had then died in mysterious circumstances. He seemed to be trying to link his death with Charlotte's. Confess I thought he was jumping at shadows, but he did seem to have his feet on the ground so I talked to him . . . initially so . . . but after a while I began to suspect that he had lost the plot, so to speak.'

'Oh?'

'Well, insisting that the two deaths were suspicious, a middle-aged man has a massive stroke, a woman gets deliberately run off the road by a vicious joyrider – tragic yes, but hardly premeditated murder. I failed and still do fail to see the link.'

'Did you think there was anything unusual in Charlotte selling her house like she did?'

'Nope—' Woodgate smiled and gently shook his head – 'I can't say there was, not with Charlotte. With Charlotte everything and anything was possible. She left home when she bought a monkey for a pet.'

'A monkey?' Ventnor smiled.

'Yes . . . not a big one, not a chimpanzee which is appar-ently five times as strong as a grown man and would be potentially very dangerous, but a small one, a species of small ape. It used to run round this house screeching, terrifying me and the dogs and forcing the staff to quit in droves. You can't house-train a monkey and so the damn thing wore nappies all the time and it was given to tearing the nappy off when it got uncomfortable and throwing it at people, contents included. Eventually the relics—'

'Relics?' Ventnor questioned.

'My parents, our parents . . . no longer with us but Charlotte and I used to refer to them as the "relics".'

'I see.'

'So eventually they had had enough and said, "It's the ape or us", and Charlotte chose the ape, Maximillian by name, known as "Max", probably the right decision. She was twenty at the time and off she went, and she never returned, it was just Christmas cards for the next thirty-five years. So with Charlotte, anything was possible. Her house wasn't worth much, a new build bungalow, no provenance, unlike this house. This house would be a real loss for our family. I inherited it and will bequeath it to my eldest son and he to his, so long as the dynasty is extant . . . but, back to Charlotte. Frankly I couldn't see the advantage of her releasing the equity in her house at her age, mid-fifties, thirty years of life in her; she'd be penniless at the end of it all. The amount of equity she would have released wouldn't have kept her going for thirty years and the house would belong to someone else. Equity release plans could only be of interest to folk who are on their last legs, getting radiotherapy or chemotherapy to extend their life for another twelve months. Such a person, if they were alone in life might say, "Well, OK, I'll sell up now and give away the cash but live here until I croak".' He paused. 'Yes, I can see the attractiveness of selling up in those circumstances but not when you are fifty-six or fifty-seven and in good health. It just doesn't add up and deliver.'

'What did your sister do for a living?'

'Not a lot. The business world and the family firm was not for her, except at a low level. She could have carved a niche for herself in the typing pool but not in the board-room. She just didn't fire on sufficient cylinders to survive on the board. She would have been a liability for the company. She was head in the clouds, airy-fairy. She went off to live the hippy life in Goa for a few months, that's where she picked up the idea of a monkey for a pet. She tried painting, tried to write poems but it didn't put food on the table which is what it is all about at the end of the day. When she died she was working for a company that made toys.'

'Toys?'

'Toy parrots.'

'Parrots?' Carmen Pharoah gasped.

'Gaily painted outlines of parrots, cut out of a thin piece of plywood, made so that they would perch on the edge of a table. They sold them at craft fairs or from stalls at folk festivals, bit sad if you ask me, but that was Charlotte.'

'It doesn't sound as if she could generate the sort of money you'd need to buy a house?' Carmen Pharoah commented.

'She couldn't.' Woodgate glanced at her briefly, but only briefly. 'She is of this family, the relics bought her the bungalow and she had shares in the firm and received an annual dividend, if she still had shares, she might have sold them as well as the bungalow, Charlotte being Charlotte.'

'Who would we talk to about Charlotte?' Ventnor asked. 'Who would know her well, especially in the last months of her life? It doesn't sound like she was socially isolated.'

'No, she wasn't socially isolated; she mixed with some harmless sort of weirdos who made parrots. You should try "Parrots and Co."'

'Parrots and Co?'

'Well, that's what I call them. I have their business card; Charlotte sent one in a Christmas card.' Julian Woodgate levered himself out of the armchair with some difficulty, revealing, by doing so, that he was not in the best of physical condition. He had sat down without difficulty when Pharoah and Ventnor had been shown into the room by a butler, evidently called Horace, but standing proved difficult for him. Once upright and balanced, Julian Woodgate padded out of the room and returned a few minutes later with a small business card which he handed to Ventnor. 'There you are,' he said, 'Vale Folk Art. They even have a phone number.'

'Thank you.' Ventnor slipped the card into the breast pocket of his jacket. 'Tell us, how did Mr Hoole know about Charlotte's death and the selling of her equity?'

'I was wondering when you were going to ask that question.' Julian Woodgate sank back into the armchair. 'It's crucial to the inquiry if the deaths are suspicious—' he drew on the cigarette and exhaled slowly – 'he said he was contacted by a newspaper man, a reporter who had scented a story.'

'Interesting,' Carmen Pharoah commented. 'What was his name?'

'Don't know,' Julian Woodgate smiled, 'but he works for the *Vale Free Press*.'

Keith Hoole stood and smiled broadly and extended his hand as Hennessey strode confidently into his office. 'Mr Hennessey.' He spoke warmly, taking Hennessey's hand in a firm, but not overfirm grip.

'Thank you for seeing me at such short notice.' Hennessey took his hand.

'No problem, please take a pew.' Hoole indicated the chair in front of his desk.

Hennessey gladly accepted the offer and sank into the reclining 'executive style' chair which he found pivoted as well as reclined and fancied he could get used to such a chair in very little time. He regretted that it would not, though, be seemly in a police station. Hoole's office was, he noted, neat and well organized, a poster depicting New York City in a modern art form hung on the wall behind his kidney-shaped desk. To his left a window ran the length of Hoole's office, beyond which was a yard. Men in blue coveralls seemed engrossed in the task of lowering and securing a metal lattice-like structure on to the rear of an articulated lorry.

'It's off to Folkstone,' Hoole said, following Hennessey's gaze, 'that's what we do here at Hoole Fabrications. Come a long way since I built a garden brazier for a neighbour of my father's, then got requests for another . . . and another . . .'

'Really.' Hennessey smiled. 'Is that how you started?'

'Yes, oak trees from acorns. That is the final section of a footbridge for a road which has been widened. So, this is about my father?'

'Yes, yes, it is.' Hennessey let his fedora rest on his knee.

'Good—' Hoole reclined in his chair – 'I am trying not to be angry and I appreciate that you were not the interested police officer, but I am pleased that you, that is the police, are now thinking his death might be suspicious . . . how shall I say . . . viewing it with suspicion.'

'We are not viewing it with suspicion.'

Hoole's face fell. 'You are not? Then why are you here?'

'We are viewing it afresh, in the light of subsequent developments. We are taking a fresh look at it, accepting that it might, and I emphasize might, be suspicious.'

Hoole breathed deeply. 'Alright, I can accept that. It is at least a step in the right direction.'

'It is often the case that deaths become suspicious years later because of other, subsequent, developments,' Hennessey explained, 'and it may be that your father's death is one such. It is often the way of it.'

'I see,' Hoole growled. 'Well, how can I help you?'

'Really just a little background information. You say that you found your father's body?'

'Yes, he didn't answer his midday phone call so I drove over there and found him slumped in the chair in front of the television set. The set was not only switched on but it was on the wrong channel.'

'The wrong channel?'

'The wrong channel for him, I mean. It was probably

something else I should have mentioned, that my father always felt that he had missed out on an education in life and enrolled on an Open University Course, though he didn't take the degree, but following that, he used to rail against what he called "silly television", chat shows and games shows, soap operas or low-grade films.'

'I see.'

'The sort of stuff that's on commercial television during the day.'

'Yes.'

'My father tended to use television to feed his mind so, documentaries and OU programmes, good films and high quality drama, that was his taste in TV but never during the day, such is not on during the day anyway, but when I went round his set was tuned into commercial television and a game show was being broadcast, the sort of rubbish that gets shown to avoid a blank screen. To say that that was out of character for my father would be a massive understatement.'

'I see.'

'And I also had the clear and distinctive sense of someone else's presence.'

Hennessey nodded. 'I know what you mean there.'

'You do?' Hoole looked interested, alerted by Hennessey's reaction.

'Oh yes, don't I just. Going into a room where nothing is out of place and yet you sense "something's happened". I have experienced that sensation a few times and that atmosphere can last a long time. I first encountered it when I was a young man of about eighteen or nineteen. I turned down an alley in Greenwich South East London—'

'Yes, I know Greenwich. Is that where you come from?'

'Yes,' Hennessey replied smiling, 'from the bottom end, just off Trafalgar Road.'

'Ah . . . knew you were not a Yorkshire man by your accent. London, I got London . . . but it's Greenwich, interesting.'

'I've been up here most of my working life but I have never lost my accent, but anyway, I turned into this alley . . .

never been there before and I had such a sudden and strong sense that "something's happened here". Turned out that a murder had been committed in the alley a hundred years or so earlier, so that atmosphere had remained all that time. Believe me; my dog would not have walked down that alley.'

'So you take me seriously?' Keith Hoole held eye contact with Hennessey.

'Most certainly.' Hennessey spoke earnestly, holding eye contact with Hoole. 'Most certainly, I do.'

'Thank you, not everyone does so. I can't make everyone believe me and I am not asking it to be taken as evidence, of course I am not, but it does seem to add to the notion that foul play was the cause of my father's death.'

'Yes . . . yes . . . but only between you and me. As you say it is not something we can offer as evidence.'

'Interesting you say that, "you and me". I thought the police only visited in pairs?'

'Only when interviewing suspects or making door to door inquiries. As I said, this is more a search for background information and to meet the family.'

'I see, and it was the murder of my uncle a few days ago which has prompted the fresh look at my father's death?'

'Yes . . . in a word . . . yes.'

The phone on Hoole's desk warbled softly. He snatched it up, listened and then said, 'I'll phone them back and . . . Emily . . . you still there? OK, hold all further calls please, until Mr Hennessey leaves. Thank you.' He smiled at Hennessey. 'Sorry about that.' He replaced the handset gently. 'So, Edwin's murder, my uncles?'

'Yes, it seems that Mr Edwin Hoole was going to meet someone in respect of your father's death, or so he led his wife to believe, but he said little really, no details.'

'He wouldn't, it's just the three brothers, very secretive, but I was pleased for Edwin when he met Vivienne, she was very good for him. She's a good woman. They were very happy together.'

'We understand that there is some issue about your father selling his house? Would you know anything about that?'

'No, but it was very puzzling to myself and my brother and to Edwin. Again, the expression "out of character" comes to mind. My father was all for inheritance, hated inheritance tax, even for the super rich, though there he and I disagree, I quite like the idea of the super rich paying inheritance tax on their estates but father thought it both criminal and immoral. It's their house and land, he would argue, why should their heirs pay tax on its value when they inherit it? So it was a real surprise. I mean, it was like the world had stopped turning to find that he had sold his home some years earlier to a finance company who let him live on there. All very odd.'

'No reason at all to do that?'

'None, his photographers requisites business was doing well, really very healthy. So not only was it out of character for him to release the equity, it was without motivation. No reason to do that.'

'What was his state of mind at the time of his death?'

'I'd say that it was back to normal.'

'Back to normal?'

'Yes, he was devastated by mother's death, losing his wife like that.'

'Yes, the hit-and-run.'

'The murder-and-run, the actions of that motorist were deliberate.'

'So I understand. I have spoken to the officer in charge of the case and have visited the scene of the crime.'

'You have?'

'Yes, came here from there. Different time of the year and the footpath has now been elevated to prevent any similar accident but I saw the clear, straight road, and also its relative remoteness. I could imagine the footpath as it was when at road level, with just a few pre-war wooden posts . . . got frequent concrete ones now.'

'I know,' Hoole sighed. 'I go and lay a wreath there each anniversary.' He glanced out of the window at the crew of men struggling with the section of footbridge. 'It just wasn't the loss of his wife; it was the suddenness and the mind-lessness of it. I mean, how could a man, or woman, suddenly "give in" to the urge to run someone down just because they could get away with it? Just nudge the car off the road, at speed, on to the path, crash into someone, take the life, get back on the road and drive home, just for kicks, or perhaps my mother paid for someone else's crime in that driver's life.'

'Yes . . . it . . .' But words failed George Hennessey.

'I was once deliberately splashed by someone. A car was parked by the side of the road, engine running; beyond the car was a pool, a puddle in the kerbside, it being a wet day after a period of rainfall. I was on foot, on the pavement, and I walked past the car. Then, when I drew level with the puddle, the car accelerated and splashed me and drove off. He'd got his victim. I could only feel sorry for that driver, especially as he was alone in the car. That made it really sad, being the only occupant. But there's a big differ-ence in magnitude of the crimes between deliberately splashing someone and deliberately taking their life, though in essence it's the same crime, misuse of a motor car when in need of a victim.' Hoole shook his head. 'Sorry, I don't have the words I need.'

'But after the accident? Your father was not himself?'

'No, he was lost, devastated, didn't know where he was. I was running two companies then, his and mine. He took over again after a few months but he was never the same. Mum and Dad grew up in the same street . . .'

'Really?' Hennessey smiled.

'Yes, knew each other all their lives and Dad had travelled a smooth road up until then, maybe too smooth, maybe fate decreed it was time he hit a rough patch. It's just one of the thoughts that occur to one from time to time when I am searching for an answer. Married early and successfully, his business grew steadily over the years, no setbacks, two sons, no serious illness or tragedy in the family, so maybe it was overdue.'

'Can I ask, do you think it was deliberate?'

'The running her down? Of course it was.' Hoole became

indignant. 'What have I been saying these last few minutes? Of course it was deliberate.'

'I mean as in premeditated.'

Hoole fell silent. He stared at Hennessey. Colour drained from his face. His jaw sagged. 'That hadn't occurred to me,' he said quietly.

'Alright,' Hennessey sat forward, 'let's hang around this for a little bit.'

Hoole put his hand up to his jaw. 'Yes, I think I'd like to do that. I think that might be interesting.' He leaned forward and pressed a button on his desk and when a tinny voice said, 'Yes, Mr Hoole?' He replied saying, 'A tray of tea for myself and this gentleman, please, Emily,' and released the button before the tinny voice could answer. 'I take it that you'd like some tea, sir?'

'I'd love some, thank you.' Hennessey smiled.

'She's generous—' he indicated to the door of his office – 'especially when she is not paying for it. I am sure the tea will come with a more than plentiful supply of toasted tea cakes, or muffins, or similar.'

'Ah, I had a wholesome pub lunch in Malton but I dare say that I could find room for a little more.'

'Well waste not, want not.'

'Indeed, and we must all bear in mind that nobody's next meal is guaranteed.' Hoole and Hennessey chatted idly for a minute or two about the issue of food short-ages and the complacent attitude of Westerners towards food supply and then Hennessey asked, 'Well, if the murder of your mother was premeditated, who, if anyone, might benefit?'

'Frankly I can't think of anyone, or of anyone who would want to harm her.' He paused as the door to his office opened.

Emily, slender, black skirt, white blouse, blonde hair, did indeed bring in a plentiful supply of teacakes with the tea, and, placing the tray gently on Hoole's desk, withdrew silently.

'I am damn lucky to have her.' Hoole opened the pot and stirred. 'Damn lucky. She is the last word in efficiency.'

He glanced out of the window at the crew who still struggled with the section of bridge. 'They are making a right
dog's breakfast out of that. They are trying to put it on back
to front and the lorry driver is not amused, he just wants
to get on the road. I can't interfere, not good management,
let them sort it out, which they will do. They're a good
crew and I'll only lose them if I breathe down their necks
at every turn.' He poured the tea. 'Can't think of anyone
who'd benefit, or who'd want to harm her,' he repeated.
'Father's business had rivals but no enemies. They had no
enemies as a couple that I knew about. Her funeral was
well attended. She left little in her will. The house was in
joint names and my father became sole owner upon Mother's
death. I miss her a lot. I dare say I was lucky with my parents.'

'I am sorry.'

'Nothing to be sorry about, but thank you anyway.
Teacake?'

'Thank you.' Hennessey leaned forward and took a
lavishly buttered toasted teacake.

'Nothing to be sorry about,' Hoole repeated as he too
helped himself to a teacake. 'Better by far to have had
a good mother whose memory you can treasure, rather
than a bad mother whose memory you resent and whose
influence in your life you have to try to rid yourself of.
Even if you lose the former sort early in life and the
latter sort hangs around to enjoy longevity . . . so nothing
to be sorry about.'

'There is the suggestion that your father might have been
the intended victim. What are your thoughts on that?'

'Is there?' Hoole again held eye contact with Hennessey.
'That really is news.'

'It is something we have to now consider. It may not
have seemed relevant at the time.'

'What was not seen as relevant?'

'Both your parents being about the same height, dressed
similarly, white coats, matching his-and-hers white coats,
that is, your father in black trousers, your mother in black
slacks . . . and crucially . . . unusually for them, for no
reason, your mother was, that night, walking on the outside.

So given that, and given your uncle's recent murder, we now wonder if your father was the intended victim. That it was premeditated murder, not a spiteful act of road rage.'

Hoole put his half-eaten teacake slowly down on his plate and glanced to his right and the team of men by then lashing the bridge section to the lorry, having turned the thing round as Hoole had promised, at the building beyond his yard, and the ploughed fields beyond the building and out to the sky beyond and above the fields.

'So,' Hennessey pressed, 'who would benefit from your father's murder?'

'No one—' Hoole looked appealingly at Hennessey – 'nobody that I know . . . really.'

'So, no lead there, it would appear?'

'I wish I could help you. I really do.'

The two men sat in silence eating the teacakes and sipping the tea.

'Clearly had more room that I thought—' Hennessey put his crumb-laden plate on Hoole's desk – 'despite the lunch. The haddock was of passing succulence.'

'Really? Which pub?'

'The George and Dragon, lovely old pub, panelled walls, low beams, peat fire . . .'

'Peat?'

'Yes, softer warmth than coal, very cosy.'

'Yes, I came across pubs with peat fires in Ireland, but didn't know about the George and Dragon. I must try it.'

'You will not be disappointed. So, when did your father sell the equity in his house?'

'Shortly after mother was killed, so I found out when he died. You know, I never made the link. He must have signed on the dotted line when he was still in a state of shock,' Hoole groaned, 'a high pressure salesman exploiting his vulnerability. Whether accident or murder, my mother's death left my father in a suggestible state of mind and when he recovered, he didn't tell us what he had done. He must have been too ashamed. He left us his business and we sold that, so he did leave me and my brother Andrew . . . he lives in London . . . he did leave us something, but he must have been too ashamed to tell us what he had done with the house.'

'To whom did he sell the equity?'

'To an outfit called 541 Finance, Investment and Security Limited. They're in the Yellow Pages.'

Thomson Ventnor and Carmen Pharoah both thought the man to be typically 'folksy'. He had a nervous disposition, speaking quite rapidly, as if his real feelings were buried but buried shallowly and he was fighting to keep them subsurface. The man was slight of build and had a thin, bony body. He stood in the middle of the floor of the small lock-up in which was a wooden working bench. Sheets of plywood lay stacked up against the wall. In a large crate beside the plywood sheets were scores of plywood pieces cut out in the shape of outlines of parrots, ready to be painted. The finished articles, about thirty in number, were perched on a shelf which ran along the length of the further wall. The lock-up smelled of paint and sawdust and new wood. It was difficult for both officers to see the man, Henry Miles, by name, surviving in the mainstream of life. He was, thought the officers, a man of desperate and aching vulnerability. His schooldays could not have been easy for him. He said, 'Charlie painted the parrots. Oh goodness, yes, Charlie painted the parrots. I do it now, but Charlie did it . . . when she was alive . . . goodness, yes.'

'What sort of woman was she?' Ventnor asked.

'Charlie? Just a nice girl. She was good at painting, very good . . . very neat . . . very good.'

'Were you and she close?'

'Close?'

'Friends or lovers?'

Miles shook his head. 'Goodness, no, she worked with me here in the winter and in the summer we'd tour the folk festivals. We'd go to Whitby, which is the big one up here and then all the way to Dorset and Cornwall and faraway places like that. Oh goodness, yes.'

'Selling parrots?' Pharoah restrained herself from smiling.

'Oh goodness, yes, children liked them.'

'I see.'

'We travelled in Reg's camper van. They would sleep in the van and I would sleep in a tent beside the van with the dog when we had him.'

'Reg?'

'Charlie's boyfriend . . . well, man friend.'

'Where do we find Reg?'

'The garage in the village. There's only the one garage, Parr Autos it's called. Goodness, yes.'

'Far?'

'Ten minutes by foot.'

'Is it alright to leave the car here, outside your workshop?'

'Yes—' Miles nodded vigorously – 'plenty of room.'

The ten-minute walk transpired to be nearer twenty but it was not at all an unpleasant experience for both officers, offering a relaxing stroll past tidy cottages with overgrown privet and proud lawns awaiting the first trimming of the season, between freshly tilled fields of rich, brown soil, with early wild daffodils and crocuses growing in the verge and nest-building birds flitting in and out of the hawthorn hedgerows. The village of Alderton Green revealed itself to be small and compact. Probably just too large to be called a hamlet, it had an open area surrounded by houses, a food shop, two pubs and Parr's Autos.

Ventnor and Pharoah stepped off the lane as they reached the village and onto the pavement that they followed to Parr's Autos which was a small establishment, just one corrugated iron shed in front of the two dated-looking petrol pumps, red with a white glass globe on top. Soothing sounding classical music came from within the corrugated iron shed, the officers followed the source of the music and entered the shed, within which was a man in overalls underneath a car which was raised up on a hydraulic ramp.

'Mr Parr?' Ventnor asked.

'No, but I'll be with you directly,' the man replied with a grin as the music from Mozart's *Horn Concerto* changed to Vivaldi's *Four Seasons*. The man clearly had his radio tuned to Classic FM. Ventnor and Pharoah waited as the man tightened a nut with a great deal of effort. He then emerged from under the ramp smiling and wiping his hands on a cloth. 'Can I help you?'

'Hope so.' Ventnor showed his ID. 'Police.'

'Oh.' The man looked disappointed, thought the officers, though not guilty or crestfallen. He had nothing to hide.

'Sorry,' Ventnor said smiling, 'did you think we might be customers?'

'Yes, I hoped that you were, business is slow. The motor trade tends to slump a little in the winter months. There's just a lot more private car usage in the summer, so that means more servicing, more repairs, more petrol sales.'

'I see, well there's no trouble . . . but you are Reg?'

'Yes, but not Parr.'

'No?'

'No, Parr's Autos was the name of the garage when I bought it. It had a good reputation so I kept the name and fortunately I kept the customer base. Kept up the good service and the customers keep coming back, but not in the sense of complaining, I don't mean that, just good, regular customers who brought their cars to Jerry Langley, who bought the garage from old Freddy Parr when he retired and I bought it from Jerry when he retired. I'll be selling it soon; I can see sixty-five on the horizon. I don't want to be working when I am old enough to receive a State Pension. That is in three years' time, so if you know someone who wants to buy a going concern, a repair garage, good customer base . . . do all the cars in the vicinity, no close competition . . . sell all the petrol, reasonable price . . .'

Ventnor smiled and shook his head. 'Sorry, I don't know of anyone who might be interested but should I happen to meet someone like that, I'll mention your name.'

'Appreciated. How can I help you? I am Reginald Oliver, by the way.'

'Charlotte Woodgate.' Pharoah spoke with a serious tone.

The man's eyes closed briefly. The name clearly caused him some emotional pain.

'Oh—' he glanced up at the low, grey sky – 'yes, Charlie, she was my partner. We never married; Charlie just wasn't one for marriage. A bit too, dunno really, Charlie just wouldn't settle with anyone, that was Charlie and her ape.'

'Max, yes, we heard about him.'

'He was just as much a character as she was, better than a guard dog. Used to leave him in the lock-up at night, I tell you he'd defend the garage against a company of paratroopers. I didn't allow him in the house; there was this issue with his nappies—'

'Yes, we heard about that also.'

'So, when Charlie was staying over at my place, we'd leave him in here. You know, a bed to sleep on, plenty of food and water. She was distraught when Max died. She really was closer to that ape than any human. Had me build a coffin and we dug a grave and raised a stone over it in a wood near here . . . it's still there . . . a stone sticking up out of the ground amid the trees, moss-covered now but Charlie and I, we were like two ships on each other's horizon, but sailing in company despite the distance. It suited both of us but we were still an item. Neither of us wanted the on-top-of-each-other closeness of marriage. We both needed plenty of space. Well, I'll be on my own now, no more partners for me at my age but at least I'm alive. Charlie was in her fifties, healthy . . . a bit flighty . . . but healthy.'

'Flighty?'

'Her feet just were not on the ground. She was painting parrots when I met her.'

'Yes, we have just come from the workshop.'

'Hobby shop more like, can't call that work, but you've met Henry Miles and his multinational corporation, cornered the marked in painted parrot cut-outs? Well, Henry is a lot like Charlie but Charlie had more about her than that, a lot more, but the mainstream of life just wasn't for her or Henry. She just wasn't a Woodgate. It's just impossible to visualize her in a smart business suit with a PA and an Audi sports car, but give her a pet ape and some parrots to paint to sell at folk festivals . . . well, she was a very happy camper then.'

'I see.'

'She said once that her parents started out ballroom dancing and ended up all-in wrestling and if that was marriage, you could keep it. So why the interest in the late Charlotte Woodgate, spinster of this parish?'

'Developments.' Carmen Pharoah didn't want to give too much away. 'We need to talk to someone who was close to Charlotte.'

'Yes, yes, I dare say I was, I dare say you could say that.' Oliver raised his hand in greeting as a car drove by travelling out of the village. 'Customer,' he explained. 'But, yes, I dare say that I was as close to Charlie as she would allow anyone to get close to her. Certainly she seemed closer to me than to the pompous Julian who sits around all day in a smoking jacket while a manager looks after the company for him.'

'We are interested in her will,' Ventnor explained, 'especially in connection with her property, the bungalow she owned.'

'Well, that's it, she didn't own it, she had sold it before she died to some equity release company but that was Charlie. If you knew her, once you got to know her, then nothing came as a surprise. Selling the equity was the sort of mad thing she'd do.'

'You think? I mean, you think it mad?'

'Yes, at fifty plus, only fifty plus, you don't release your equity that early in life, but Charlie was eccentric, dare say that's the word, better word than flighty. In fact come to think of it there was a fella asking the same questions a few weeks ago, a journalist geezer.'

'Oh?'

'Yes, he gave me his card. I tossed it because I had no use for it.'

'Oh.' Pharoah allowed her disappointment to be heard.

'Eric Breathnyck.' Oliver smiled. 'Remember the name because there was a boy in our class of that Christian name and the surname is so unusual that I remembered it, Eric Breathnyck of the *Vale Free Press*. I read "the press", so I had no need to keep the card. A nice fella . . . a bit weasel-like.'

'Weasel-like?'

'In terms of his attitude, ferreting away, single-minded, dog-with-a-bone, he seemed quite excited, as though it was his ticket to Fleet Street.'

'Eric Breathnyck,' Pharoah wrote on her notepad, '*Vale Free Press*.'

'That's it.'

'Thanks.' Ventnor smiled. 'We'll pay a call on him. But thanks a lot; it's a helpful bit of information. Thank you.'

Hennessey settled into the chair in front of Commander Sharkey's desk. Sharkey, a small man, small for a police officer, was, as usual in Hennessey's view, impeccably dressed in a three-piece suit and tie. His desk similarly had an 'everything in its place' quality about it with little cluttering the polished work surface. Behind Sharkey were photographs; one of his wife and children, another of Lt Sharkey in the uniform of a British Army officer and the Royal Hong Kong Police, as was. Sharkey listened patiently as Hennessey gave a verbal report on the progress of the Edwin Hoole murder.

'So perhaps earlier and linked murders?'

'Yes, sir.' Hennessey glanced out of the window of Sharkey's office; the view was of roof tops of the nineteenth-century terraced houses behind the police station. 'I'll get fully up to date tomorrow morning at the overview session in my office.'

'Good.' Sharkey paused. 'So I have nothing to fear?' He tapped the photograph of himself when in the RHKP with his fingernail.

'I am sure of it, sir,' Hennessey smiled reassuringly.

'It wasn't corruption as we know it here in the UK, just a sort of negative corruption. I never bribed witnesses or planted evidence or took money to do something. I would just be told by a sergeant not to patrol a certain area at a certain time – I didn't, and there'd be a brown envelope full of folding green in my desk drawer the following morning. It was that sort of corruption. I wasn't there very long, a few weeks only, just long enough to see what was going on and what I had become part of, then I resigned.'

'Yes, sir.'

'But if such was happening here . . .'

'I am sure there is nothing to worry about.'

'I hope you're right, George. It would destroy me . . . and this police station.' Sharkey sat back in his chair. 'So how are you, in yourself?'

'Fine, thank you, sir. Getting used to the desk and keeping the overview.'

'Good. You know the story of Johnny Taighe, good man, maths teacher, good at lower school maths but just when he should have been allowed to soft-pedal to a deserved retirement, what did they do but give him senior school maths to teach. He was overweight, smoked like a chimney, big red nose, so he was hitting the bottle in the evenings, he was a heart attack waiting to happen . . . and happen it did. That's not going to happen on my watch.'

'I am alright, thank you, sir, well on top of things, do not feel under stress, have a pint of brown and mild most evenings in the pub but I do not hit the bottle at home and I don't smoke. I think it's a safe bet that I will reach retirement and if I don't, it won't be because of the job.'

'Good.' Sharkey gave a rare smile. 'Good. I am gratified to hear it. Good.'

At home that evening, Carmen Pharoah ate a ready-cooked meal and then had a warm shower, after which she wound herself into her late husband's towelling bathrobe and was saddened to notice that the thing seemed to be falling apart. It was just one more item that had belonged to him which she would also soon be losing. She lay on her bed in her flat on Bootham, listening to the sounds of the night; the 'ee-yor' of a train passing through York Railway Station, the high-pitched whine of the high revving diesel engines of the buses, a solitary woman in heels, click-click-clicking her way home, the good-humoured shouting of a group of young men, university students by their cleanliness of speech and upper-middle-class accents, she guessed. How different it had all been still just a matter of months ago. A few months ago, she and her husband from St Kitts, both determined to overcome prejudice, both working for the Metropolitan Police; she a Detective Constable, he a civilian employee, an accountant. Then at work, a colleague, pale-faced and worried-looking took her into an anteroom. It must have been quick they said, he couldn't have known anything. The heavy goods vehicle came from nowhere and crushed his car. After the funeral she just needed to get away from London. She wanted to be punished for surviving and the hard, cold north seemed perfect for banishment. She would return to London. At some point. But not for a while yet. Her sentence must be served. In full.

Thomson Ventnor went home to his modest three-bedroomed house in Bishopthorpe. He also heated up a ready meal, but unlike Carmen Pharoah he dressed in a lightweight Italian-designed suit and a topcoat and went out. He took a bus to the outskirts of York and then strolled up a leafy lane and turned into the grounds of a Victorian mansion and opened the front door. Within he was immediately met with a blast of warm air, unhealthily warm, he always thought and, opening his coat, he went upstairs to a room where elderly people sat in chairs against the wall. A television set attached high on one wall was switched on and its sound flooded the room. A man, sitting in the far corner smiled with delight as he recognized Ventnor, but in the time it took for Ventnor to cross the room to the elderly man, the man had, in his mind, retreated into a trance-like state but Ventnor knelt beside him and said, 'Hello, Dad,' nonetheless.

Ventnor then took a bus into York and went to a pub, The Hole in the Wall on High Petergate and from thence, at 11.00 p.m, to the Augustus Night Club where he got into conversation with a woman who had somehow shoehorned herself into a size twelve dress from which Ventnor thought she would burst at any moment. They had, they found, much in common, both being divorcees. He bought her a drink and another, and another . . . but eventually went home alone.

Again.

It was Thursday, 01.15 hours.

FIVE

Thursday, 11 February, 09.10 hours – Friday, 12
February, 02.27 hours
*in which much is learned of the Whispering Woods Murder
and Somerled Yellich and George Hennessey are at home
to the kind reader.*

Hennessey placed his elbows on his desk top and
rested his chin in his palms. 'That's interesting. Isn't
that interesting?' He smiled at Carmen Pharoah and
Thomson Ventnor, noticing the latter seemed to have blood-
shot eyes. Another late night he surmised. 'So, you two
have had mentioned to you the *Vale Free Press*, and you
have a name, one Eric Breathnyck.'

'Yes, sir,' Carmen Pharoah replied sharply. Ventnor just
nodded, as if, thought Hennessey, reluctant to speak.

Yellich sat cradling his mug of tea with both hands. 'The
only two crimes so far are the murder of Edwin Hoole just
the other day, and the death by hit-and-run of his sister-
in-law some years ago. That's manslaughter . . . possibly,
and both may be caused by the victims just being in the
wrong place at the wrong time, and Charlotte Woodgate's
death, the car accident, the result of aggressive driving . . .
again manslaughter, possibly, all possibly unconnected and
their selling their homes to an equity release scheme, just
coincidence.'

'Yes—' Hennessey sipped his tea – 'point taken, that is
indeed one end of the spectrum and I do not think that we
should lose sight of that. You're right. But . . . but—' he
held up his index finger – 'but equally, we should not close
our minds to the possibility that something considerably
more sinister is afoot here. We remember that Mr Edwin
Hoole was sufficiently concerned about his own safety that
he insisted on meeting Julian Woodgate in an out-of-the-

way pub in an out-of-the-way village. He might have been being a little melodramatic, a little too cloak-and-dagger, but again, equally, to use the word again, equally, he might have had good reason to be cautious. There's an awful lot of smoke about, as I have said before, an awful lot. How are we fixed for manpower, Sergeant?'

'Well, all the team is present, sir, as you see, no absence caused by sick leave, no other high-profile cases. Burglaries on the increase and also car crime, from, rather than of, satellite navigation equipment is being targeted. Beer off's are being robbed, possibly by the same gang, but all fairly petty compared to this.'

'Alright, so we are coping.'

'Yes, sir.'

'Ventnor, what are you working on apart from the Hoole case?'

'I picked up the non-fatal stabbing at the racecourse, sir. I believe I am close to an arrest. I feel confident. I am also the interested officer in respect of the fatal RTA on the bypass, a drunken joyrider. I'll be sending a report to the CPS any day now. The joyrider is still unconscious and may be brain-damaged . . . so it's a bit messy. He killed two people and may be a vegetable for the rest of his life. So it's a bit of a waiting game, that one. Other than that I have nothing to get in the way of the Hoole case.'

'Good man.' Hennessey turned to Pharoah. 'DC Pharoah?'

'Domestic violence cases, sir, fairly petty by comparison. Vandalism on the Hessle Road Estate believed to be a gang of juveniles under the influence of alcohol and other controlled substances. I have the names of one or two to be interviewed and some CCTV footage to sift through. I have arranged for an increase in uniformed patrols on the estate and that seems to have calmed things for now at least. It frees up time to give to this inquiry.'

'Webster, what are you doing?'

'Car crime also, sir, but unlike DC Ventnor's, this crew is highly organized. They seem to be stealing top-of-the-range vehicles to order. One owner tells of an ex-army officer being involved, but that might be a separate case. It doesn't follow the same pattern. No violence against the person as such, but an awful lot of money is involved and the insurance companies are clamouring for a result because, at the end of the day, they are the victims. I also have the death of a down-and-out on Heslington Common but I think that will be deemed to be natural causes or misadventure. Poor old guy just seems to have laid down in the rain and died, possibly during the morning frost. No signs of a struggle, empty stomach and a half-empty bottle of fortified wine in his coat pocket. He most probably just lay down and went to sleep for the last time. So I also have time to devote to the Hoole murder inquiry.'

'Good. Sergeant Yellich, your caseload?'

'Well, space as well, sir. I have the case of the barman who walked out of The Junction in Holgate but that is just a question of waiting for him to surface.'

'He took the till takings, if I recall?'

'Yes, sir. Strange really, the statements read like temporary loss of sanity rather than a premeditated crime, but the barman was on his own on the Monday night of the week, which is the quietest night and on which night the pub landlord and his wife go out with friends and apparently stop over at their friends house in Driffield. Anyway, about ten p.m. the barman just empties the till into a holdall, tops up the holdall with cigarettes and a bottle of spirits and then tells the customers to help themselves, saying he has switched off the CCTV, and which some of them did. The majority of punters finished their drinks and went home but the younger element of the customers stayed . . . and the party went on until a foot patrol noticed the pub appearing to be doing good business at two o'clock in the morning, but of course it wasn't doing any business at all.'

'Indeed.'

'I have the Benefit fraud as well, but that is cut and dried. Six blokes went into the dole office in working clothes and footwear, caked in fresh mud. Heavens, they may as well have had "just popped off the building site" written on their jackets . . . but they are pleading guilty, so just the paperwork to do. Then I'll send the file to the CPS. So I too have space.'

'Good, good, so we can give our all to this. I had my regular chat with the commander yesterday. He's concerned about my health, good fellow he, so you'll be doing the legwork. So, as DC Pharoah says, we could be looking at four murders. So today, DC Webster and Sergeant Yellich, go and visit the *Vale Free Press*, talk to Eric Breathnyck.'

'Yes, sir.'

'He sounds like he has a story to tell. Find out what it is.'

'Very good, sir.'

'So—' Hennessey leaned back in his chair – 'we seem to need to know more about the smaller finance companies who do business in the Vale and especially about those who are moving into equity release schemes, like the 541 Company. They are one, but there will be others. So, Pharoah and Ventnor, you two can do that . . . Work through the Yellow Pages and visit as appropriate. See how far you get. For myself, if there is an "iffy" finance company, I think I might know a man who can tell me about it.'

Breathnyck and Yellich shook hands warmly and smiled at each other.

'Please—' Breathnyck indicated the chairs in his office – 'do take the weight off your feet.'

Yellich and Webster sat, as invited, and both officers read a cramped office, a desk top of loose papers and folders, walls lined with shelves upon which books had been placed in no particular order, some flat, some upright, some, inexplicably to Yellich's mind, placed with their spines innermost to the wall. The office had a musty smell and Webster thought that an open window and a tended potted plant would not go amiss; either in fact would be more than welcome. Breathnyck himself was a short man, dark hair, bearded, dressed in a corduroy jacket, jumper, open-necked shirt, faded and threadbare denim jeans. 'It's all I can offer, hardly *The Times*, but it's all I have.'

'Thanks anyway.' Yellich adjusted his position on the wooden upright chair. 'Strange name.'

'Mine or yours?'

'Both.' Yellich grinned. 'I dare say they both are.'

'Well, dare say it's much the same for you, but we know little . . . East European. Don't know when the ancestor or ancestors came to the UK or what the original name was but it was clearly altered a little to make it more accessible to western ears. I have considered anglicizing it further by deed poll, so long as it begins with a B. Something classy like "Broomhead" to be pronounced "Bromhead", to give my sons an easier time of it.'

'You don't strike me as the sort of person who'd give in to fashion,' Yellich observed, 'the editor of a Free Press, I mean.'

'Well, my sons are twins, just six months old, so I have some time yet, but my father told me he pondered doing the same thing, to give me an easier time of it but when it came to the crunch he didn't, because he felt like he'd be betraying his ancestors. Dare say I'll feel the same. So Joshua and Isaac Breathnyck they will be.'

'I have pretty much the same story,' Yellich said. 'Eastern European, we think Czechoslovakia . . . anglicized somewhere down the line but not fully so, just to make the name accessible to British ears.'

'Any children to inherit it?'

'One,' Yellich answered solemnly, 'but he has special needs so it won't be such an issue for him.'

'Oh, I am sorry.'

'It's one of those things. Anyway, you haven't been going long?'

'The paper? Just a few years, and I am it; the editor, chief reporter, cub reporter, photographer, manager, accountant. We have correspondents from all over the shire who file reports and we generate an income of sorts from advertising and from sales.' Breathnyck grinned. 'We had to educate the public on that, Yorkshire being Yorkshire . . . where copper wire was discovered when two Yorkshire men fought over a penny. Folk thought "free" meant "free" as in a "free sheet", so-called, the sort that gets pushed through your letterbox, so they walked into newsagents and walked out with a copy of the Free Press without paying for it and the newsagents had to run after them saying "it's not that sort of 'free' paper". It has an unfettered voice but you still have to pay for it.' He paused. 'But we are surviving. So, how can I help you?'

'We understand you called on a gentleman by the name of Woodgate?' Yellich asked. 'Julian Woodgate?'

'Pompous creep . . . but yes, I did. Why, has he made a complaint?'

'No, he hasn't. We also believe you contacted the Hoole family?'

'Oh.' Breathnyck looked crestfallen and sank into his chair behind his old wooden desk. 'You know, I think I know where this is going. I assure you I have no evidence, nothing I can bring to the police. I know the rules of the game, as soon as I had any evidence I would have come to you.'

'Yes, though even suspicions must be reported, but carry on, please.'

'Well, perhaps I should have contacted you but it is a narrow path, a narrow dividing line, and we chase a story until we have evidence and then we are obliged to notify the police . . . but without that sort of actual evidence the press can keep running with the ball. I can be prosecuted for withholding evidence, but not for withholding suspicion. So, when we are still short of hard evidence, we can keep burrowing away. A scoop is every editor's dream and this sort of scoop could really establish the *Vale Free Press*. Our circulation would skyrocket, the advertising revenue would come in . . . the snowball effect you see, and since I have a family to support, well, I would defend my sources and my secrecy to date should you choose to issue proceedings.'

'We won't because you have no evidence, as you said, so unless we discover otherwise, there will be no action taken against you but your name was mentioned in the course of our investigations into the murder of Mr Edwin Hoole.'

'Yes, I read about that incident, attacked in the street a few nights ago . . .' Breathnyck's voice trailed off.

'Are you realizing something, Mr Breathnyck?' Webster pressed.

'I hope . . . Oh . . .' Breathnyck's voiced failed.

'You see, it might have been better to come to us with any concerns and suspicions. If Mr Hoole was murdered to silence him, once you had started asking questions . . .' Yellich shrugged. 'Such things happen.'

Breathnyck covered his mouth with his right hand and looked at Yellich with widening eyes.

'So, if you'd just tell us what you know, Mr Breathnyck.' Yellich sat back in his chair as Webster took out his notebook and pen. 'You could perhaps tell us how you became interested, or involved.'

'It was a phone call—' Breathnyck spoke with a soft air of resignation – 'dare say it was the phone call started it. A man phoned me, wanting to meet me. He said he had a story, a story about the Whispering Woods murder.' Yellich's brow furrowed. 'The elderly lady?'

'Yes, found with her head smashed in.'

'I remember it.' Yellich turned to Webster. 'You must remember it too, you live quite close to the scene of the crime.'

'I do . . . we do . . . often exercise our dog there. I wasn't on the case though; the skipper thought I lived too near . . . but . . . no result anyway.'

'No, it's a cold case, didn't get anywhere with it, no motive that we could detect, no enemies, just a lady in her sixties, recently retired, enjoying her retirement, and healthy, beaten ferociously about the head, found by a dog walker a few hours after it had happened but he didn't see anything. We thought she had crossed the path of someone with murder on his mind. But no leads and so it was a cold trail, even just a few hours after the event and it was already a cold trail.'

'Well—' Breathnyck leaned forward and rested his arms on his desk top, creasing papers as he did so – 'the man who phoned me, the informant, he told me that there was a motive.'

'Really?' Yellich raised his eyebrows.

'Yes, really.' Breathnyck smiled. 'He told me that she was murdered for her money.'

'We didn't think she had any, not so much to murder for, though one man's fortune is another man's loose change. People have been murdered for a pocketful of coins before now.'

'I was told that her murder was linked to the deaths of Harold Hoole and Charlotte Woodgate.'

'Do you know why this gentleman, your informant, didn't come to us?'

'Not for definite. I got the impression that he didn't like or trust the police and I also paid him for his information, not a great deal but more than you would have given him.'

'Can't argue with that point,' Yellich growled.

'He was also anxious that the *Vale Free Press* should have the story, not a provincial or national paper . . . felt that the little man deserved a chance at the big time. He said he always supported the underdog, so I got the lead.'

'So what did he tell you?'

'Rather you asked him, this is all getting too much for me.'

'Name and contact details? Give us those and we'd be delighted to make his acquaintance.'

'Delighted,' Webster echoed, his pen poised over his notepad.

'Robin Eyre,' Breathnyck read from the card in the card index in front of him. 'I only have his telephone number . . . never met him. We did plan to meet and he gave me his address but I seem to have lost it, just have his telephone number.'

'That'll do.' Webster smiled. 'That's all we need.'

'Can I help you?' The smartly dressed man shot to his feet with a ready smile as Carmen Pharoah and Thomson Ventnor entered his office.

'Police.' Ventnor showed his ID.

'Oh—' the man's smile faded though he retained his self-confidence and composure – 'no trouble, I hope?'

'Probably not, sir,' Ventnor replied. He thought the man

to be in his early thirties, light-grey suit, blue tie, a salesman's smile. Behind his desk was a calendar with a conservative and tasteful photograph of an English village scene. The office itself was small, quite cramped, thought Ventnor, but clever use had been made of all available space, additionally helped by evident fastidious neatness. The window looked out over York rooftops with the Minster in the middle distance squatting under a low, grey sky. 'This is 541 Finance?'

'Yes, sir, 541 Finance, Investment and Security Limited. Can I help you?'

'Hope so.' Carmen Pharoah noted an overstrong smell of air freshener. 'We are making routine enquiries about the smaller finance companies who offer equity release schemes.'

'Oh, well, please do take a seat.' The man waited until the officers had seated themselves in the chairs in front of his desk, then he too sat down. 'We are the only small finance company to offer such a service, in this area anyway.'

'You are Mr Cobb?' Thomson Ventnor read the name-plate on the man's desk.

'Yes, I am Gordon Cobb.'

'A strange name.'

'You think so?' Cobb's eyes narrowed as if stung by the remark. 'Nobody has remarked on it before, plenty of Cobbs in the telephone directory.'

'Sorry.' Ventnor smiled. 'I meant 541 Finance.'

'Ah—' Cobb relaxed – 'it's nothing more than the location of York in terms of its latitude and longitude . . . fifty-four degrees one degree north, west . . . that is approximately. The city is a few miles to the south-west of that precise grid reference but it's sufficient for a name of a York-based company.'

'I see, interesting. Is it an old company?'

'Ten years, about.'

'Are you employed or a partner?'

'Oh, a lowly employee, I'm afraid, recently appointed, only been here for about eighteen months.'

'I see, so still finding your feet?'

'No, settled in now, it's getting routine, but the company is growing and has healthy reserves.' He smiled confidently. He had ginger hair, neatly cut. 'And I hope to grow with it.'

'What does the company do?'

'Well, finance . . . it's a finance company.'

'Such as?'

'Loans, for example, we loan to folk when or where a bank wouldn't. We advise on buying stocks and shares—' Cobb seemed puzzled by the question, as if it was obvious what a finance company does – 'that sort of thing.'

'I see, and what about equity release? Do you do that?'

'Yes—' Cobb smiled proudly – 'that is also part of our service, as I said, a small part, but a successful part so far, although it is a recent development.'

'How does that work, in a nutshell?'

'Oh—' Cobb stroked his chin – 'well, very simply really. If someone owns their home, mortgage fully paid off but is short of cash then we would buy their home for its market value and then rent the house back to the person.'

'Rent it back?'

'Yes, but only for a peppercorn rent. By having a rental agreement that prevents any complications arising if the previous owner claims squatters' rights, for example.'

'Alright.'

'So the person continues to live in their home and has a great deal of money now freed up and there to spend to ease their day-to-day life, buy luxuries, take extensive holidays . . . everyone benefits. When the person, the erstwhile homeowner goes the way of all flesh, then we assume vacant possession of the property and sell it for what it is then worth. There's no investment like property but, having said that, you know location and condition of the property have to meet certain criteria. We wouldn't buy a rundown house on a flood plain.'

'Understood.'

'So, like I said, all benefit. The elderly person accesses

the cash they have tied up in the house, and the company makes a tidy profit when it comes to take possession and sell it. A much better investment than if 541 put its money in a deposit account. There is some risk because the property market has its occasional slump, but it always picks up again and does so rapidly. Our equity release customers are spending the kids' inheritance. Well, so what? It's theirs to spend.' Cobb rocked back in his chair. 'We think it's a fair offer. Other much larger companies do it. In fact, as I have said, we are new in that area with our service, but equity release schemes are about twenty or thirty years old. It's the finance sector's response to Britain's aging population.'

'Is it reasonable, do you think?'

'It's not for everybody.' Cobb adopted a more serious tone of voice. 'But if the person is elderly, if they have no dependants, if they have a medical condition which will mean they will expire within twelve months, for instance, then . . . then it might be a good plan. I can see its appeal. The person gets the money to travel, see friends and family for the last time . . . globally so, and writes cheques to determine what balance goes where and to whom, though we like to obtain the property some years before the person expires.'

'Oh?'

'Yes, we make our profit by resale. If we sell within twelve or twenty-four months, we make little profit but if we can sell after a period of ten years then we make a handsome profit.'

'Would you do it?' Ventnor asked.

'In a word, "yes", depending on my personal circumstances. Alone . . . children up and gone or no dependants to leave it to, then why not use it? I, for example, have for some reason I can't put my finger on, a desire to step inside the Arctic Circle and I have a fascination with a town in Kentucky in the US called Bowling Green . . . able to go visiting places like that, cash money, I mean, there's no pockets in a shroud, you can't take it with you . . . so, "yes", I would, circumstances depending.'

'No pressure is put upon the person to leave the house prior to their eventual passing?'

'Oh . . . no . . . none, assuredly so, after all, as I said, the greater the time gap between purchase and sale, then the greater our profit.'

'Interesting.'

'Why the questions, may I ask?'

'It is merely that this company has been mentioned once or twice during our investigation into a . . . well, it has been mentioned.'

'We felt we needed to take the measure of you,' Carmen Pharoah added with a smile. 'But we are also calling on other finance companies.'

'I see.'

'How many such properties do you have on your books at the moment?' Ventnor asked.

'Not many compared to the really big finance companies, only about twenty, if that. I can obtain the exact figure for you, if you wish, but I assure you, everything is above board.'

'Thank you,' Ventnor nodded. 'That would be useful.'

'Have you made any recent sales?' Carmen Pharoah asked.

'Of houses we have earlier purchased? Yes, we have.'

'We are interested in the sale of the property once owned by Charlotte Woodgate and also the property owned by Harold Hoole.'

'Oh, yes?'

'You know the properties in question?'

'I know of them. The equity release is not really my area of responsibility but I have heard the partners talk about those properties . . . both sold because of unforeseeable accidents, I believe.'

'Yes,' Ventnor replied coldly. 'So who does deal with that part of the business?'

'Mr Malthouse and Mr Bagnall, the founders and the MDs of 541.'

'Are they in?'

'Not at the moment. In fact they are out looking at a

property at the moment. Don't expect them back today at all—' Cobb glanced at his watch – 'the property is out near Hull.'

'We'd like to look at all the files you have in respect of all the equity release work this company has done, both past and present.' Ventnor spoke suddenly.

'The MD's won't like that, they would insist on a court order before releasing them. I mean, for myself, I would be happy . . .'

'Yes, alright—' Ventnor stood, as did Pharoah – 'we will get one.'

'I'll tell the MD's you called,' Cobb stammered. 'I'll tell them.'

'Yes, please do.' Carmen Pharoah smiled. 'We'll see ourselves out.'

'Robin Eyre?' Yellich asked casually. 'Is he in please?'

'No.' The woman had a harsh and a rasping voice and instantly reminded Yellich of the time when, as a young man, he went into a backstreet car hire firm to find the receptionist sitting in front of a desk top of empty beer bottles. 'Heavy night last night?' he quipped, only to receive the reply in the same sort of harsh, rasping voice, 'No, son that was my breakfast.' This present lady was no alcoholic, that was plain, but her voice was similar. 'She is though,' the woman added. 'I am she. Robyn Eyre. Robyn with a 'y', being the female version of the name.'

'Ah . . .'

'And my voice—' she laughed nervously – 'well, I can't help that, it's a medical condition. I often get mistaken for a man by folk who only have voice contact with me.' She shrugged. 'My parents told me they wanted a boy, hence my name, so maybe they got less of a girl than they feared.' She leaned against the side of the front doorway of her small house in Holgate, black terraced houses, where washing hung in the street, motorcycles were chained against lamp-posts and where stood The Junction pub where a few days earlier the duty barman had absconded with the till

takings and bottle of spirits allowing the patrons to help
themselves, some of whom did, until chanced upon by a
police foot patrol in the early hours of the following day.
Holgate was a part of the city of York not visited by tourists.
'Police you say?'

'Yes. Mr Breathnyck of the *Vale Free Press* gave us your
name and telephone number.'

'And from that you can find an address. I am ex-directory.
Unlisted.'

'Police have reverse telephone directories; entries are
listed in numerical order against a name and address.'

'Interesting, I never knew that. Dare say you learn something each day. So, you've found me . . . now what?'

'Mr Breathnyck told us that you had tipped him off about
a crime which may have been committed,' Yellich advised.
'Ring any bells?'

'Merrily on high.' Robyn Eyre stepped backwards into
her house. 'You'd better come in; the curtains in the street
are beginning to twitch anyway.'

Robyn Eyre's home revealed itself to the officers to be
kept in a neat and tidy manner and had a strong smell of
furniture polish and air freshener. Yellich and Webster and
she sat in the front, 'best' room of the house, the window
and door of which abutted the pavement requiring lace
curtains to be hung in front of the window, though Yellich
was to observe that whenever a foot passenger walked past
the house, no attempt to peer within was ever attempted.
The houses at either side of the narrow road similarly also
valued the privacy offered by lace. On the walls of the room
were framed photographs of women in naked or semi-naked
posses. Robyn Eyre followed the officer's gaze and smiled
and said, 'Like I said, my parents got less of the girl they
feared, but they don't know about that bit.' She indicated
the photographs on the wall. 'They live in Leicester. They
don't visit me and I don't visit them . . . cards at Christmas
and birthdays and that's it. Ours is just one of those families.
We are fragmented.'

'Sorry, to hear that.' Yellich smiled softly. He found
himself liking Robyn Eyre, denim-clad, mid-thirties. He

thought and believed that she would be a source of credible information. She had, he felt, that essential honesty about her. 'So what can you tell us?'

Robyn Eyre smiled and reached for a pipe which she began to fill with tobacco from a pouch. 'Lots,' she said, 'lots and lots and lots, but I assume you mean what can I tell you about 541?'

'Perhaps,' Yellich replied. 'You tell us if you suspect anything.'

She lit the pipe with a match and played the flame over the bowl. 'This doesn't help the voice,' she said, 'but so what? I'll play the hand I am dealt. What can I tell you? Nothing . . . nothing for sure . . . no evidence of anything—' she drew on the pipe with evident satisfaction – 'just suspicion.'

'Good enough.' Yellich spoke in what he hoped was a reassuring tone. 'It's often the way of things, a voice of suspicion, of concern, a thin wisp of smoke; it's all it needs to be to trigger an investigation. Tell us what you suspect and we'll take it from there.'

'Very well.' Robyn Eyre sat back and crossed her legs, resting her right ankle on her left knee and once more savoured the pipe tobacco. 'I used to work at 541, just secretarial work but I didn't fit in.'

'It happens.'

'I was told that the company has a high turnover of staff so I don't lose sleep over it.'

'That's interesting, and good for you.'

'Yes,' Webster nodded slowly, 'that could be significant.'

'Story was,' Robyn Eyre continued, curling her finger lovingly round the stem of her pipe, 'that 541 wanted a secretary, like yesterday, and the Job Centre sent me round to see them, so I wasn't the dolly bird they were looking for, and hoping for, but they were not in a position to pick and chose so I got the job. I was only there a few weeks when I started to hear things, I mean overhear rather than be told.'

'Yes, things like . . .?'

'The two boys, young men, and also the woman who came in from time to time, never knew their names . . . and

I worked in the adjacent room to Mr Bagnall, one of the owners and Managing Directors. I wear contact lenses and it seemed that when my eyesight began to fail my hearing became keener, it became noticeably more sensitive. Time and time again in my life I have heard things that other folk have not heard. Once, I was walking in the country with some friends and we saw a lot of hot air balloons coming towards us and I said "I can hear them", when they were still some distance away and my friends scoffed and didn't believe me but I could hear the gas jets hissing and whooshing and then as the balloons got nearer my friends then also heard the same sound, and in Scotland once I heard the echo of a train's horn, really in the distance and I said, "It's coming, it'll be here in about ten minutes", and again my claim was greeted with derision because all else was silent save for a birdsong or two. As we waited on this remote platform on a single track line, but then, what should arrive ten minutes later, possibly fifteen . . . I had heard the echo in the glen.'

'I can believe you,' Yellich said, and Webster smiled and nodded but said nothing.

'I had a man friend once,' Robyn Eyre continued, 'that was before I decided that girls are for me, and he told me that when he started to go bald, at that moment his beard started to grow much more strongly. The human body compensates for the loss of one sense by increasing the strength of other senses. So it seems anyway.'

'I have heard the same,' Yellich agreed.

'The point is that no one believes I have the hearing I do in fact have, and so when I was tapping away on the word processor, I often used to hear what was being said in the next room, sometimes softly but still with the door open, and paper-thin walls helped, or didn't help, depending on your point of view. They helped me to hear things that I was not supposed to hear. They could hear me tapping away on the keyboard as they spoke in a whisper, assuming I couldn't hear but often, very often in fact, I heard every word. That happened quite a few times and most of what I heard was just day-to-day business, but occasionally, when the boys or the woman or all three visited, then I heard things that were, well, shall we say "iffy".'

'Things like?' Yellich coughed as strong, rich-smelling tobacco smoke teased the back of his throat.

'Phrases like, "Well, we got away with it but we can't do that too often", and "If the law starts asking questions, then we really are in trouble", and what else did I hear? Oh, yes, "Why would they link them, they're accidents", and all in hushed but excited voices.'

'I see—' Yellich cleared his throat – 'interesting.'

'Then, what was it that Mr Bagnall said? "We need another one, things are getting tight". Such phrases I overheard from time to time over the few weeks that I was there.'

'I see.'

'Oh, yes, and another time I heard Mr Bagnall saying, "It's costly, Whispering Woods really cost us".'

'Whispering Woods really cost us,' Webster repeated.

'Yes, that's what he said. I don't know what he meant but then I heard Mr Malthouse, the other owner and director, say, "Yes and we had to pay for the Smeaton woman".'

Yellich and Webster glanced at each other.

'Don't know what they meant but it just sounded suspicious.' Robyn Eyre glanced out of the window as the high-visibility-jacket-wearing postman walked slowly past. 'No delivery for me today. If there was, it would only be junk. What mail that does arrive always arrives at midday these days. All the important mail is sent by fax or email so there's no point in the old postie getting up at the crack of dawn any more to deliver junk mail.'

'None at all,' Webster echoed.

'So what happened then?' Yellich refocused the interview.

'Oh—' Robyn Eyre looked at Yellich – 'well, I didn't know who the "Smeaton woman" was and so I accessed the file on the computer, easiest thing in the world. I was given the password you see.'

'Do you still have it?' Yellich asked eagerly.

'"Bluesky", but it won't do you any good; they change the password each time an employee leaves.'

Yellich sighed. 'I thought it was too much to hope for. So please, carry on.'

'So I accessed the file on a lady called Smeaton and found out that 541 owned her house. They had bought it from her some little time before she died and then upon her death they had sold it but not for much profit.'

'Do you recall her first name?'

'Georgina . . . same name as my sister so I remembered it. Robyn and Georgie. My poor parents really wanted boys. Georgie got married and has two daughters, so my parents haven't even got grandsons, poor they.'

'Georgina Smeaton?'

'Yes, in her sixties when she died and lived outside York . . . and she was murdered.'

Webster nodded. 'Yes, the Whispering Woods murder.'

'Yes, I read about it at the time, didn't make the connection until I read the file. Murdered in the woods but her house was also ransacked, all the valuables were taken; silver, jewellery, robbed right and clean she was.'

'Yes, it was what we know as a "cold case",' Yellich said, 'probably about to be heated up.'

'I do hope so, that lady deserves justice. Sixty is not old, not these days, and not for a woman. Well, it was then that I left. I was getting cold-shouldered out and things didn't feel right, so I phoned in sick and then phoned in and told them I wouldn't be coming back at all.'

'You didn't come to us?'

Robyn Eyre shook her head. 'No, not directly, didn't think I had enough, but I did contact the *Vale Free Press*. I released the virus of suspicion that way, and it worked, it has reached you, as I hoped it would.'

George Hennessey climbed into his Burberry and screwed his fedora down tightly round his head and left the police station at Micklegate Bar and walked the walls to Baile Hill and thence across the city to Speculation Street, and the Speculation Inn at the bottom end of the terrace of houses. He stooped to enter the low doorway and turned immediately to his left and entered the snug of the pub, within which was a hard bench that ran round the edge of the wall, six round tables with chairs in front of each, a serving hatch, but not a bar. Light came in through frosted glass on which was etched, 'Sanders and Penn's Fine Ales' Shored-Up sat in the corner furthest from the door and serving hatch. He smiled briefly at Hennessey.

'You look despondent, Shored-Up.' Hennessey took off his hat and placed it on the bench. He walked to the serving hatch and ordered a whisky and a soda water and lime. He carried the drinks back to where Shored-Up sat and placed the whisky in front of him.

'You don't know how welcome this is, Mr Hennessey, so welcome.' Shored-Up grasped the glass with long, slender fingers and lifted it to his lips.

'So what's the problem?' Hennessey sipped the soda water and lime.

'That Miss Pratt. Who else? Who else?' Shored-Up moaned. 'An interview with her is like doing ten rounds with a bare-knuckle prizefighter, just one session and my head is spinning.'

'You are not avoiding the appointments with her, I hope? Remember you are only at liberty now because I put in a good word for you and you promised not to let me down.'

'I have not, and I will not let you down, Mr Hennessey. I will attend all interviews, and I had one such very bruising encounter this very forenoon. I didn't realize how lucky I was with my last probation officer who didn't mind if I missed the occasional appointment and wanted to talk only about the fly-fishing he was going to do when he retired.' Shored-Up raised his glass. 'God bless him.'

'Miss Pratt is only doing her job, Shored-Up,' Hennessey growled, 'and she seems to be doing it very well.'

'Such a contrast though, Mr Hennessey.'

'Between the two probation officers, yes, sounds like Miss Pratt is good for you.'

'Probably, but it isn't comfortable and also there is the

contrast between her appearance and her attitude, such a young, attractive woman. I am old enough to be her father. Such sweet-smelling perfume, it made me go all gooey inside when I met her and then received such a punishing discussion. Doesn't raise her voice or anything like that, just questions this and questions that. So young and she can't be manipulated.'

'Good for her. Sounds exactly what you need.' Hennessey sipped his drink.

'You might think that, Mr Hennessey, but it is sapping my confidence and business is bad enough as it is. Mind you, I have just found a most agreeable hotel where many elderly ladies take afternoon tea, seeking companionship and conversation. Such agreeable gentlefolk, Mr Hennessey, such agreeable gentlefolk, and the service there is excellent.'

'I see, and no doubt Lt Colonel Smyth of the Devon and Dorset Regiment is now frequenting the hotel also?'

'Of course, a man has to live, and it's Lt Colonel (retired) if you don't mind.' Shored-Up smiled.

'Of course, you are a little long in the tooth to be a serving soldier.'

'Indeed.'

'Any victims of late?'

'None, I assure you, none.'

'I do wish that was true. We have reports of a Rolls-Royce and other expensive cars being stolen, as if to order, one of my team is the interested police officer.'

'Really?' Shored-Up raised his eyebrows.

'Yes, really and the description given by the lady owner is of a retired army officer, slight of build, courteous of manner. She is one Mrs Trent, Madeline Trent.'

'Oh, yes, dear Madeline, such a sweet soul.'

'But you did not steal her car which she allowed you to borrow from time to time?'

'Oh, Mr Hennessey, how could you? In fact I was with her when her car was being stolen.'

'So it was you?' Hennessey shook his head. 'I should have known.'

'Well, you would have found out anyway, but yes, her Rolls-Royce was purloined but I do have a cast-iron alibi. I was with her. I drove her to the races and was with her throughout the afternoon and when we returned to the car park, her lovely old car was gone, a Silver Shadow, high mileage but those cars don't age.'

'But you drove it?'

'Yes. She disliked driving, she much preferred being driven.'

'I meant, you have driven it alone, in her absence?'

'Yes, but only upon her invitation. I never asked to borrow it.'

'So how does it work? Once in possession of the keys it is the easiest thing in the world to have a spare set of keys copied. Is that it?'

Shored-Up glanced up and out of the window. 'Looks like rain.'

'So you sell the spare set of keys for a thousand pounds and tell whoever where the car can be found, like the car park of York Racecourse and it is removed while you and Mrs Trent are watching the galloping horses. It was insured for fifty thousand pounds. An Arab in the Middle East would pay twice that . . . nice little earner. In fact a thousand quid for the keys seems cheap.'

Shored-Up smiled but said nothing.

'You'll be recognized by the owner of the shop who cut the spare keys. He won't cut Rolls-Royce keys every day.'

'Oh, I don't think so, for one the shop wasn't in York, it was over on the dark side. I wouldn't soil my own nest.'

'Lancashire!'

'Yes, and between you and me I might have paid a lad to take the keys for me and get them cut, can't afford to get caught on CCTV. I won't be admitting to anything, and Madeline collected the insurance. Everybody wins.'

'Except the insurance company.'

'Oh, and they can't afford it? I tell you, Madeline was more indignant about having to ride home in a lowly taxi than she was about the theft of her Rolls-Royce. Must be nice to have that sort of dosh, but I didn't tell you that.'

Shored-Up drained his glass and pushed it across the table top toward Hennessey.

'Whoa—' Hennessey held up his hand – 'I need something from you, Shored-Up.'

'You do? And I thought you had just popped in to be sociable, to pass the time of day.'

'Unfortunately not . . . no . . . we are getting wind of something.'

'Oh?'

'Yes, an outfit called 541, a finance company here in the famous and faire.'

'Have not heard of it.' Shored-Up pursed his lips. 'It does sound right up my street though, but I know not the name.'

'All in connection with the murder of Edwin Hoole which you may have read about.'

'Yes, well heard about courtesy of the television.'

'And the possible suspicious death of his brother and sister-in-law some years earlier, up to now believed to be natural causes and an accident, but now seen as suspicious and the murder of a lady in Whispering Woods out by Selby way.'

'That rings bells.'

'Yes, it was well publicized at the time but all the victims had some connection with the 541 Company.'

'Smoke.' Shored-Up smiled. 'I see the way your mind is working.'

'So what can you tell us?'

'Nothing, but I could visit the den.'

'If you could, we have ways of showing our gratitude, as you have found out.'

'Yes—' Shored-Up nodded – 'I know, a blind eye here, a good word there. Yes, I will contact you if and when I have something for you.'

'My mother's murder?' Tim Smeaton laid the paintbrush across the top of the tin and stepped off the ladder. 'Just touching up a bit.' He indicated the window frame. 'Noticed the paint was getting thin, just an extra coat to get it through the remainder of the winter. I'll give it a proper new coat in the summer. They say you must paint your house once every ten years. It's been fifteen years since this house was last painted . . . but my mother's murder? Is there some new information?'

'Possibly,' Yellich replied. 'We just have a few questions.'

'Well, in that case, I'll stop for the day.' Smeaton took the paintbrush and plunged it into a jar of white spirit and pressed the lid firmly on to the tin of paint. 'Let's go inside.' He peeled off his gloves and stepped across the front threshold of his house, inviting Yellich and Webster to follow him. 'Felicity! Felicity!' Smeaton's voice echoed in the modest semi-detached which was his home.

'Yes?' The answer came from the upper floor of the house.

'Police . . . it's the police.'

'Police?'

'Yes, nothing to be alarmed about, it's in respect of my mother.' He turned to Yellich and Webster and softly told them. 'You'll have to excuse Felicity, she's highly strung, things like this set her off easily. She hasn't always been like this. I hope it's a phase. I hope she'll get better, get back to being like she was when we were first married. But, please come in.' Smeaton led the officers into the back room of the house, which the officers noted was neatly kept but also with evidence of children in the home; a pile of toys on the floor in the corner of the room and paintings, clearly by children, attached to the walls at child height with a sort of 'I-did-this-and-it-goes-here' attitude. The rear window of the house looked out onto a small garden which was also neatly kept and with a child's tricycle resting on its side in the centre of the lawn. Beyond the back fence of the garden could be seen another similar house in suburban Dringhouses, York.

'Please,' Smeaton smiled, 'do take a pew.'

The officers sat down as invited, Yellich in an armchair, Webster on the settee.

'So—' Smeaton sat in the other armchair – 'what can I help you with?'

'Well—' Yellich leaned forward and rested his elbows on his knees, clasping his hands together – 'we have reviewed the case file we have on your mother's death . . . her murder . . . Mrs Georgina Smeaton, murdered and robbed.'

'Yes.' Smeaton grimaced. 'That is the injurious thing, it really is, the excess of violence. He or they took her rings, her handbag, her brooch from her coat lapel, in fact anything of value but he . . . or they need not have taken her life and what they stole wasn't worth a great deal. She was a bit frail but she had all her marbles. She had it all there inside her head, her brain was as sharp as a tack. She could have lived quite a lot longer, it wasn't her time. Mind you, I dare say it never is in the case of murder.'

'She was assaulted out of doors?'

'Yes, in Whispering Woods near her home which is near Selby.'

'Yes.'

'But it was suspicious that she was out at night.'

'At night?'

'Yes, it's all in the file.'

'Sorry—' Yellich felt embarrassed – 'I only gave the report a quick glance.'

'I see.' Smeaton smiled. 'That at least sounds promisingly urgent. I do hope so. You see, we phoned at nine p.m. each night . . .'

The door of the room burst open and a small woman with a wide-eyed expression ran into the room. Tim Smeaton sank back into his armchair with evident embarrassment. 'My wife,' he explained, a little needlessly so, thought Yellich and Webster. 'Felicity, those are police officers.'

'Mrs Smeaton.' Yellich stood, as did Webster.

'Trouble, there's trouble.' Felicity Smeaton spoke in a high-pitched voice. 'The children, the children, what's happened?'

'No trouble at all, Mrs Smeaton,' Yellich spoke calmly.

'All safe and sound.' Tim Smeaton placated his wife. 'Please, do sit down, gentlemen. Felicity, why don't you make us a tray of tea?'

But Felicity Smeaton planted herself firmly and determinedly on the settee next to Webster and was clearly not going to be moved. She wore her hair in a bun, an ill-fitting dress and well-worn carpet slippers. She had a fearful, timid manner, thought Yellich who felt that living with her could not be easy and was wholly sympathetic to Tim Smeaton's hope that her present attitude was a 'phase'.

Smeaton continued, 'We phoned her at nine p.m. each evening, just before she retired for the night. She tended to turn in at nine thirty p.m., she didn't keep late hours.'

'Yes.'

'So all was well at nine p. m. that night . . . and then the following morning we had a call from the police, her body had been found in the woods by a dog walker who knew her and was able to identify her to the police . . . a Mr Darby, a very kind-hearted neighbour, a figure in my child-hood and who has known my mother for years. It was quite upsetting for him.'

'So your mother left her home some time after nine p.m. when she would normally have been preparing to sleep for the night?'

'Yes, very unusual. And it was about this time of the year too, a dark, cold, wet night when the only folk who are out are those who have to be out of doors. Not like Mrs Jepson, another of her neighbours who lost her marbles and who went out at night in her dressing gown and stocking feet at all hours and in all weather after putting her husband's meal on the table for him. Her husband having died ten years previously but Mum was all there, she didn't go walkabout . . . never . . . even in midsummer.'

'I get the picture.'

'Her house keys were taken but her house wasn't broken into. She had nothing of value in the house, didn't keep her life savings in an old shoebox under the bed, nothing like that. She had money in the bank and up to her death I thought all her money was in her bricks and mortar but after her death we found that it was in the bank.'

'We'll come on to that in a moment.'

'Good. Good—' Smeaton set his jaw firm – 'because that's the real mystery. I tell you, that is the real puzzle.'

'Alright, so it was wholly out of character for your mother to go walking at night.'

'As I said, and not in those weather conditions. You know, I couldn't help being annoyed by the police, dismissing her murder as an opportunist robbery gone wrong. I mean, what felon waits for a victim in a rainswept woodland at night? Muggings take place in city centres and dark streets.'

'Yes.' Yellich nodded in agreement. 'I can understand your anger . . . and I apologize for the police.'

'My mother was not in the wrong place at the wrong time. Somebody, some person wanted her dead but and it's a big but . . . but she had no enemies, none at all. She was just a widowed lady living alone. My father was a civil servant; a very low-grade civil servant too, no frills in his life at all. He managed to pay off his mortgage before he retired and for him, that was a great achievement. We never had a car, that was a luxury beyond our dreams, and no foreign holidays. Mother went out to work as soon as me and my brother were school age. So who, who, I ask you, who would target an elderly lady with a background like that?'

'What sort of personality was your mother?' Yellich asked.

'Quiet, I'd say. She kept herself to herself.'

'Was she strong-willed?'

'No, no she wasn't. She had double-glazing installed, which she didn't need, and a new door as well, which she also didn't need, just gave in to high-pressure cold-calling salesmen . . . and it seems she sold her house . . .'

'Sold it?' Yellich queried.

'Yes, she signed some agreement; she'd get the money the house was worth but could remain living in it, paying a modest rent. Again, she didn't need that; she had an index-linked pension to live on after father's thirty-five years in the civil service.'

'Who did she sell the house to?'

'A company called 541 something.'

'When did you find out about the sale of the house?'

'Not until after she died. It was confirmed, to my dismay, at the reading of the will, but I first found out about it when

I was clearing the house and a smooth-talking fella arrived and just started wandering round the house. Just walked in, calm as you please. I said, "Who the hell are you? You just can't come into someone's house like you own it" and he said, "Well, actually I can because I do own it." Then he told me that my mother had sold the house to his company some ten years earlier, and in that time the house had tripled in value. It was a boom period for the property market and he wanted his money. The money she had received for the house was still in her account, she hadn't touched it and she seemed to have sold it for less than its market value, so me and my brother didn't get a third of what we other-wise would have inherited, we got nearer a quarter and we had to share that. I got angry with her about the new door and the double-glazing so I think she dare not tell me she had sold the house . . . it would have been too late anyway. I couldn't have taken Power of Attorney because she was fully compos mentis. It was her house and she had every right to sell it, but it came as a real blow. First her murder and then the discovery that she was worth only about a quarter of what she would have been worth if she hadn't sold her house but once she had signed the papers and accepted the cheque, there was just no going back, no going back at all.'

'No going back at all,' parroted Felicity Smeaton. 'No going back.'

Snow started to fall as Yellich drove home that evening. Not a worrying large and sudden fall, but more in the manner of what Yellich thought the weather forecasters on television would call 'a light dusting'. He halted his car outside his small, new build house in Huntingdon and as he did so Jeremy ran to meet him, arms outstretched and Yellich prepared himself for the impact of the loving twelve-year-old. Inside the house Yellich saw instantly that Sara had been crying. She turned and held on to her husband and burst into tears again, sobbing that she was sorry 'but he's been impossible'. Yellich changed into casual clothing and took his son for a walk in the snow, which by then had

lain sufficiently to permit snowballs to be made, thus giving
Sara Yellich a much-needed hour to herself. Later that
evening Jeremy Yellich impressed his father by being able
to tell difficult times like eighteen minutes to three and
seventeen minutes past eleven.

Somerled and Sara Yellich had known the disappointment that all parents feel when told their child is not of
normal intelligence and that he has 'special needs', but
over the years they had grown to love their son who just
gave and gave and gave . . . and a whole new world opened
up to them as they met parents of similar children and
joined support groups. With luck, they were told, and love,
and patience, and stimulation, Jeremy could achieve the
mental age of ten or twelve by the time he was twenty
years of age, live a semi-independent life in a hostel where
he could prepare his own food, if he wished, but staff
would constantly be present, if only in a supervisory
capacity. Also employment for him would not be out of
the question with an approved and properly vetted
employer. From a sense of great disappointment for the
Yellichs had grown a sense of great fulfilment.

George Hennessey lay abed listening to the sounds of the
night, the owl which lived close by, an aeroplane, and
then piercingly, the sound of a motorbike being driven
cautiously, presumably because of the snow and the sub-
zero temperature, he assumed, along the Thirsk Road,
past his house, towards Easingwold. As always, the sound
of the motorbike transported him back to his childhood
home in Greenwich and terraced Colomb Street, near the
Ship and Billet pub, now renamed to his dismay as the Frog
and Radiator. He was taken back to being eight years
old, and loved helping his older brother Graham clean and
polish Graham's beloved Triumph, of how Graham would
take him for a run on the machine, with him sitting on the
pillion, his arms gripping Graham's waist. The run round
Blackheath Park, or, if Graham was feeling more adven-
turous, or more kindly disposed to the young George, then
he would drive up to London, crossing the river by Tower

Bridge, and then back across Westminster Bridge and home. It was just at that time that Graham had disappointed his parents by announcing his intention to leave the safe job at the bank and train to be a photographer. Then there came that fateful night when George lay on his bed listening to Graham kick his machine into life, and then drive away along Trafalgar Road towards the Cutty Sark, and straining his ears to catch every last decibel of the sound as Graham climbed through the gears until all sound of him was lost and replaced by the sound of ships on the river, and the Irish drunk labouring up Colomb Street, reciting his Hail Mary's. Then the sound of the policeman's knock which he would come to use, tap, tap . . . tap . . . the hushed voices followed by his mother's wailing and his father coming up to his room to tell him that Graham had ridden his bike to heaven, 'to save a place for us'.

Then the funeral, like that of his wife some twenty years later, was in the summer. He had seen then how incongruous was a summer funeral, to stand there watching the coffin being lowered amid flowers in full bloom, and flitting butter-flies and the soft jangle of 'Greensleeves' coming from a distant and unseen ice-cream van. He was grateful that not one, but both of his parents died in the winter of the year, the stillness and silence of his father's funeral and the sudden flurry of snow which lifted the young priest's cassock as he intoned 'earth to earth . . .' A winter gives to a funeral, he believed, just as summer gives to a wedding.

Often he wondered what sort of photographer, what sort of man Graham would have become. Graham, he recalled had a passion for justice and truth and would have become a photojournalist, exposing what needed to be exposed. He would not have become a sleazy paparazzo or a fashion photographer, pointing his lens only at fortune and fame and beauty. Graham would have put his own life at risk in war zones; he would have been that sort of photographer. He would also have been a good husband to a lucky woman, a good father to some lucky children and a good uncle to his nephew, Charles.

Unable to sleep, George Hennessey rose and walked to

the window of his bedroom and looked out across the landscape. A break in the cloud cover had enabled the full moon
to illuminate a winter scene of black trees and a white
blanket covering the ploughed fields beyond the garden. He
watched as a fox crossed the field, nonchalantly it seemed,
moving from left to right of his field of vision. Enchanting.
He thought the scene enchanting.

It was Friday, 02.27 hours.

SIX

Friday, 12 February, 07.05 hours – Saturday, 13
February, 11.47 hours
*in which Reginald Webster is at home to the urbane
reader and felons work for themselves.*

The shrill peep-peep-peep of the alarm jolted Reginald
Webster into a sullen wakefulness. He lay awake for
a few moments in the darkened room, listening to the
steady tapping of drizzle on the windowpane at the other
side of the drawn curtain. He only seemed able to sleep at
night if he shut the world out. Beside him his wife stirred
and reached for her watch, clipped the face open and 'read'
the time with her fingertips. She then rolled over towards
him and laid her arm gently across his chest and gave a long,
low 'can't-we-just-stay-here-all-day' moan. Webster squeezed
her shoulder with an equally gentle, 'you-know-I'd-love-to-
but', sort of response. He levered himself out of the bed and
showered and shaved and dressed and went downstairs to
the kitchen where Terry had already stirred and met him with
a tail wagging response, but as with all guide dogs, he didn't
bark loudly nor jump up at Webster. Webster made himself
a coffee and carried a second mug up to the still half awake
Joyce. He doubted that she would be sufficiently awake to
drink the coffee but the gesture was, he felt, important. He
made a bacon sandwich for himself and against all the rules
of what is good for dogs, gave Terry a rasher of fried bacon
as well. Donning hiking boots, he pulled a reluctant, long-
haired Alsatian into the drizzle and took him for a fifteen-
minute walk in the woods near his house. Webster enjoyed
the walk although he was a little saddened that the snow had
thawed in the night because he knew from previous experience that walking in silent predawn snow-covered woodland
has a mystical quality. Apart from distant lights he and Terry

on such occasions could be the only man and dog in all England. An early walk in the summer is equally pleasant but he felt it lacked that special magic of early morning in a snowy midwinter. As he and Terry walked with each other, with Terry in a distinctly protesting head down attitude, similar to the attitude of George Hennessey's dog in such circumstances, he thought again how humbling was Joyce's courage. Losing her sight in a car accident while studying fine art at university and considered herself lucky because she was the only one of the four occupants to have survived. She faced her life's new lot with stoicism and determination, managing almost anything that a sighted woman could manage and bitterly disappointed that he would not allow her to prepare hot food during the winter months, but he was insistent. He returned home and once in the kitchen of their home, Terry shook himself vigorously, pushed his way into the living room, and lay in front of the gas fire that Webster lit to warm up the house prior to Joyce rising. He made both himself and her a second cup of coffee. He carried her coffee upstairs and replaced it where he had left the first and which, as he had anticipated, had remained untouched. He kissed his wife and told her he would be back that evening and that, more importantly, he loved her deeply and dearly, and received a low purr in reply.

'Comments?' George Hennessey glanced round his team, Pharoah, Webster, Yellich and Ventnor as they sat in front of his desk. Then he looked out of the window of his office as dawn rose over the city's walls. 'Anyone?' He sipped his tea, holding the mug in his meaty left hand.

'Seems that all roads are leading to Rome, sir.' Yellich also sipped his tea, though he held his mug in both hands.

'In the form of 541 Finance, you mean?'

'Yes, sir.' Yellich raised his eyebrows. 'All arrows point to it.'

'Conjecture?' Hennessey appealed. 'Anyone?'

'Well—' Yellich shuffled in his chair – 'it seems that the only beneficiaries to all the deaths is the 541 Company. They acquired the houses, the property of the deceased prior to their deaths, and that's the motive, a very suspect equity release scheme.' Yellich paused. 'It's suspect because the people concerned, the victims, were all very badly advised to take part in such a scheme and also seemed to be approached by 541 when they were emotionally vulnerable in some way, very recently bereaved in one or two cases. As it has been stated in this inquiry, equity release can be a useful thing for people in certain circumstances; someone fighting a losing battle with an incurable illness and has no dependants. I can see the advantage of equity release in such a set of circumstances . . . you can't take it with you, release it to spend or give to whom you want to give it to while you're still alive. It's yours to spend, you've earned it. ER does have its place and a very valuable place too.'

'But not in the case of these murders, or suspect deaths.' Hennessey also sipped his tea. 'Is that what you are giving, in a nutshell?'

'In a nutshell, yes, sir, as you say, in a nutshell. Mr Edwin Hoole seems that he might be the exception. He had no involvement with 541. He didn't sign up for their ER scheme but he was asking questions about 541.'

'Yes, so that's Mr Harry Hoole's murder, Charlotte Woodgate's death and Mrs Harry Hoole's death, both in car-related accidents which may be deliberate. Forcing Charlotte Woodgate's car off the road and the running over of Mrs Harold Hoole, making it look like an opportunist hit-and-run, and then there is Mrs Smeaton's murder of some years ago in Whispering Woods . . . so three murders that we know of, plus two suspicious deaths, all connected in some way to 541 Finance.' Hennessey paused.

'And those are the deaths we know of, sir,' Ventnor offered.

'Good point—' Hennessey smiled at him – 'this could well be the tip of an iceberg. In fact you have just talked yourself into a job, Ventnor.'

'I have, sir?'

'You have, sir. You and Pharoah. Go and talk to the manager of 541. What's his name . . .?'

'Mr Cobb, sir,' Yellich advised.

'Yes, you didn't get the impression he was involved in the deaths, I think?' Hennessey queried.

'No, sir, I thought he was clean and the typist, Robyn Eyre, she didn't indicate that he was involved. The top men Bagnall and Malthouse, we haven't met them yet, she seemed to think that they and two heavies are the people we should be closing down on.'

'Alright, but let's not blunder in. So Ventnor and Pharoah, go and visit Mr Cobb, you can apprise him of our suspicions, it might encourage his cooperation.'

'Yes, sir.'

'We need the details of every case in which the 541 Company has acquired property as part of their equity release plan, especially those outside our area. Then contact the police in those areas and see if they can link murder or suspicious deaths to any of those addresses.'

'Yes, sir.'

'For myself, I called on my confidential informant. I did that yesterday. He's ferreting for me. Too early to hope for anything from him just yet, but he's come up with the goods before. So, Yellich and Webster . . .'

'Yes, skipper?'

'I want you two to call on the MDs of 541, Bagnall and Malthouse.'

'Yes, sir.'

'But at home. See what you see at their home addresses.'

'Yes, sir.'

'Time to stir up muddied waters. Let's put the cat among the pigeons.'

'We don't know where they live, sir,' Webster appealed.

Yellich threw Webster a pained expression, 'Companies House,' he said softly. '541 is a limited company, it will take a phone call. Just one phone call.'

'Oh.' Webster seemed to crumble under the awkward feeling of embarrassment.

'We can also get the information to you.' Carmen Pharoah smiled encouragingly. 'In fact we'll let it be the first question we ask of Mr Cobb.'

*   *   *

Cobb paled as he listened to Carmen Pharoah read the home addresses of Bagnall and Malthouse into her mobile phone for the edification of Yellich and Webster.

'The same information is contained in the records at Companies House,' Ventnor explained. 'You haven't betrayed a confidence by giving us their home addresses. Nothing for you to worry about.'

Cobb nodded. 'Yes, I am aware of that but this . . . this is . . . I don't know what it is.'

'It's multiple murder, that's what it is,' Ventnor replied as Carmen Pharoah completed her call and snapped the mobile phone shut and slipped it into her chunky handbag.

'They're on their way.' Carmen Pharoah glanced at Ventnor, then she turned to Cobb. 'Where are Messrs Bagnall and Malthouse now, do you know?'

'Viewing a property . . . in Doncaster,' Cobb replied with a shaking voice.

'That's convenient.' Webster smiled. 'We'd appreciate confidentiality about this, Mr Cobb.'

'Of course—' Cobb breathed deeply – 'even though I am putting myself out of a job, but for this I am willing to do that. I can get another position easily enough. I can provide good references, a good work record and a good reason why I left this post. So, all the files in respect of the Equity Release aspect of the business?'

'If you wouldn't mind,' Ventnor replied.

Cobb leaned forward and tapped the keyboard of his computer; he read the screen and said, 'More than I thought.'

'More!' Pharoah gasped, 'How many more?'

'Seventy-five,' Cobb said flatly, as if reeling from a punch.

Ventnor groaned, 'Seventy-five,' he repeated.

Cobb forced a smile. 'It's not as bad as all that, the number of equity release contracts we have, of those only twenty-two have thus far matured.'

'Matured?'

'541 has acquired the vacant possession and has sold it or is about to sell it. In other words, the previous owner is now deceased.'

'I see, and the properties belonging to Mr Hooles, Miss

Woodgate and Mrs Smeaton are among the twenty-two so-called "matured" contracts?'

'Of the other nineteen properties, how many are in the City and Vale region?'

'Let's see . . . just two . . . the other seventeen are in neighbouring areas, up in Newcastle, over in Hull, two in Sheffield . . . others in Lancashire.'

'Can we have details of the two matured contracts in the Vale, please?'

'Mrs Hay (deceased)—' Cobb read the details from the screen – 'of 163, Woodman's Croft Rise, Selby and Mrs Glenville of 272 Chaffinch Beck Lane, Wetherby.'

Carmen Pharoah wrote the addresses in her notepad. 'Thanks, we'll check this out; see if there is anything suspicious. When did they "mature"?'

'Six and eight years ago respectively.' Without being asked, Cobb clicked on the print icon on the screen and the details of all the seventy-five properties representing the sum of 541's equity release business portfolio were delivered into his tray. 'Informed consent,' he said as he handed the details of the properties to Carmen Pharoah. 'The addresses marked with an asterisk are matured.'

'Thanks.' Carmen Pharoah took hold of the sheets of paper. 'What was that you just said? Consent something . . .'

'Informed consent. It's a legal term. My brother is a solicitor, he and I were talking about this issue some time ago and he explained that a contract can be deemed null and void if one party was not fully informed of the implications of whatever it is they are agreeing to. It's a legal statute designed to protect people who are suffering from whole or partial dementia but it has wider implications. Giving consent is not sufficient; a person has to give *informed* consent. They have to have been fully informed of the implications of whatever agreement they are entering into. Consent is insufficient in itself to be legally binding . . .'

'It has to be informed consent.' Ventnor finished the sentence for him. 'That is interesting; it could be very useful to some of 541's clients.'

'It's worth taking advice about,' Cobb continued. 'If some

of those clients were not wholly themselves when they signed the contract, in a state of early bereavement, for example, then the concept of informed consent not being given could be used to help these people re-acquire the deeds to their property. They'll have to give the money back but I think many would prefer to be in possession of their property again.'

'So how did the operation work?' Ventnor asked.

'Well, as you see, the client's house is confined to the north of England, we advertised in provincial newspapers and anyone who responded would be visited by Bagnall and smoothed into signing something.'

'Not Malthouse?'

'No . . . Bagnall is the smoothie, Malthouse is a different kettle of fish, he's a hard man, hard attitude, hard, menacing voice, I can't see him selling anything to anyone, unless it's with a gun to their head. It wouldn't surprise me if he had a history. I mean a police history. He pretends to be a surveyor when they visit a house.' Ventnor and Pharoah glanced at each other. Pharoah asked, 'Do you have his numbers?'

'Numbers?'

'Date of birth,' Ventnor explained.

'Yes, I have the National Insurance details of the employees, including the MDs' on file.' Within minutes the officers were in possession of the 'numbers' of Messrs Bagnall and Malthouse.

'Well, thank you.' Ventnor and Pharoah stood. 'This is useful, and the notion of "informed consent" will be passed on to 541's clients, you can be assured of that.'

Cobb also stood. 'You know, I think I'll leave with you—' he reached for his sheepskin coat – 'I feel . . . I feel unwell, quite unwell. The secretaries can answer the phone and lock-up at the end of the day if Bagnall and Malthouse, his "surveyor" are not back by then.'

Philip Bagnall's house revealed itself to be a large, new build bungalow which stood isolated from all other buildings. It was as if, thought Yellich, as he and Webster drove up the driveway, he had bought a field, obtained planning permission and had his dream home built. Six cars were parked in a neat row in front of the house. Access to shops didn't seem to have been a concern. The nearest village was over two miles distant. Yellich and Webster climbed out of the car and walked up to the front door and pressed the bell, which caused the opening bars of 'Waltzing Matilda' to chime loudly within the house which, in turn, set a large-sounding dog barking.

The door was opened in a calm, leisurely manner by a tall woman in her forties, dressed in a grey shirt and a blue skirt. A pair of large-framed spectacles dangled from her long neck on a thin, light-blue cord. Her hair was worn in a tight bun at the back of her head. She glanced curiously at Yellich and Webster. 'Yes?' she asked, as if slightly annoyed at the doorbell being rung.

'Police.' Yellich showed her his ID, as did Webster.

'Yes?' The woman responded again in the similar indignant tone.

'Is Mr Bagnall at home?'

'No.'

'Mrs Bagnall?'

'I am she. Jessica Bagnall.'

'Can we ask you a few questions?'

'About . . .?'

'About the 541 Finance Company, about your husband and perhaps a few other matters.'

Jessica Bagnall scowled and glanced beyond the officers at the fields and hedgerows at the bottom of her garden, at the low, rain-carrying clouds and then stepped silently to one side. 'You'd better come in.'

The interior of the house was warm, too warm for Yellich's taste, as if the central heating had been turned up too high and was permanently on. He preferred a cold house with only background heating used. Webster similarly, with Joyce's agreement, switched on their heating only when their breath could be seen condensing, preferring to keep warm by the use of thermal underwear. As they entered the house a second woman, seemingly acting out of curiosity, walked strongly down the hallway towards the front door and then stopped abruptly as she recognized Yellich.

'Mrs de Vries.' Yellich smiled.

'You know each other?' Jessica Bagnall enquired with a demanding tone.

'We met earlier this week,' Yellich explained, 'very briefly.'

'Very, very briefly,' Ruth de Vries stammered, clearly very uncomfortable to have been seen and recognized by DC Yellich.

'Ruth is one of my husband's business associates,' Jessica Bagnall explained.

'Really,' said Yellich smiling, 'that is very interesting, very interesting indeed.'

'I don't see why it should be—' Ruth de Vries spoke snappily – 'but I must be going.'

'See you later.' Jessica Bagnall smiled as Ruth de Vries turned, took her coat from a coat stand and bustled past the officers, and walked away on angrily clicking heels to where a red Audi was parked amongst the other cars.

'Ruth just called to collect something and stayed to keep me company for a while,' Jessica Bagnall explained. 'Most of the time it's just me and Jasper.'

'The dog?'

'Yes. He's a mastiff, but he's kept for his bark, not his bite. A big softy, really.' Jessica Bagnall shut the door behind the officers. 'Have to keep the heat on,' she explained, 'especially on a cold day like today. Once you have the heat up, it costs very little to keep it up but to do that you have to keep the heat in.' Jessica Bagnall led the officers to a small room off the corridor which seemed to be used for receiving business, rather than social, callers. It was carpeted in a hard-wearing blue carpet, had an armchair in each corner and a small coffee table in the centre of the floor. A potted plant stood on the window sill, beyond which was the garden at the side of the house, which was little more than a grass field, so far as Yellich could tell as he rapidly scanned the room and the grounds with his practised police officer's eye.

'Please—' Jessica Bagnall indicated the armchair with a sweep of her open palm – 'do take a seat.' She sat in a chair close to the door. 'So, how can I help you?'

'Just routine,' Yellich explained, 'no need to be concerned.' He was already forming the impression that Mrs Bagnall was innocent and ignorant of any wrongdoing in respect of the activities of 541 Finance. 'Do you work for the 541 Company?'

'Heavens, no—' she smiled sheepishly at the notion of her working – 'my husband Philip, he's very traditional. He is of the view that 'man does and the woman is' and that gravitas will never attach itself to a woman. My place is in the home, his to come home to, to keep his house while he is working, doing. My anniversary presents have been things like new cutlery sets or crockery sets, to use to service him and our guests, his meal or their meals. I think it would be divorce proceedings if I so much as asked if I could take a job to get me out of the house, even a part-time post. It's just the way Philip thinks . . . but I have done well, he's not violent, I don't believe he is unfaithful and I live well. I have a generous clothing allowance and a sports car to do the shopping in and visit friends but Philip keeps me on a mileage restriction, so I can't be too frivolous with the car. I am a few years younger than my husband, well, a few, I should say nearly twenty years his junior. It's something like being married to a man who belongs to a different era, and Philip would never be persuaded to have children, that's a hole that won't be filled, not ever. Sometimes I wish I had never won that wretched competition.' She rolled her eyes upwards and sighed.

'Competition?' Yellich asked, finding the armchair surprisingly uncomfortable.

'The beauty contest.' Jessica Bagnall smiled. 'I was a beauty queen.'

'Good for you.'

'Well, not a big title, Miss Holiday Camp of whatever year it was. My father was a coal miner, there are still a few pits left in Yorkshire, in South Yorkshire, where I grew up, little place called Dinnington.'

'I have heard of it.'

'Grimy little place. He's retired now . . . my father, but that was my background. A coal miner's lass set to leave school to stack shelves before getting married to another coal miner but the beauty competition led to some modelling jobs, really small scale and all in the north of England, or opening a new supermarket or sitting on the front of a car in a bikini, or topless sometimes for a calendar, but I was seventeen and the alternative was a job in a shop, so I went with it. Paid better, more free time and I would have a long lie in bed . . . usually, and the spin-off, the social spin-off . . . invited to parties where quality people went, sometimes doctors, lawyers, but mostly they were Chambers of Commerce types with small businesses and at one party I met Philip and shortly after that I was Mrs Bagnall. I was still in my teens, just, he had a beer paunch, bald head, missing a few teeth, the rest heavily filled but he also had a Bentley and a very nice home which was bought and paid for. He was out of work when we met, having given up a job as a salesman with a big company, North Atlantic Utilities, to set up 541 with Victor Malthouse.'

'Really?'

'Yes, so he had all that money, a posh car, a big house and he was positive about life, enthusiastic, so I was a bit swept off my feet. Then I met Victor Malthouse. I didn't like Victor much, a bit creepy, sort of a violent streak about him though I never saw him get violent, but there was that potential there, just below the surface. He and Ruth got on well, though I don't envy her.'

'Ruth de Vries?—' Yellich indicated the front door of the house – 'that Ruth? The one we frightened off just a moment ago?'

'Yes, she and Victor Malthouse are partners, an item, romantically involved long-term, but not married . . . different houses but together alright.'

'And business partners?'

'Yes, they are. She has some position with 541, exactly what this is I don't know. She was divorced; her first husband was a Hoole . . . you know, the chain of photographer's requisites, everything for the discerning photographer, camera lenses, tripods, developing kit? He is a member of the family and is also related to Hoole Fabrications. They make railings and bridges and stuff life that, quite a well-to-do family.'

Yellich smiled. 'Yes,' he said quietly, 'we know.'

'Oh—' Jessica Bagnall forced a brief laugh – 'small world. My father used to say it was a small world and that it gets smaller as you get older.'

'How long has Mr Malthouse known Ruth de Vries?'

'For quite a few years, she met him while she was Mrs Hoole but exactly when they became an item, or if Victor Malthouse was the reason for her divorce from Edwin Hoole, I don't know.' She paused and glanced at Yellich. 'You know, I read in the paper that a man called Edwin Hoole was murdered earlier this week, attacked in the street it said. I didn't think, but now you are calling, asking about Ruth. It couldn't have been her ex-husband, could it?'

'Yes,' Yellich replied slowly and softly, 'it could.'

Carmen Pharoah put her phone down gently and reclined in her chair and smiled at Ventnor.

'Another one?' Ventnor commented, holding his own phone to his ear.

Carmen Pharoah nodded. 'In Sheffield. Same MO but . . . but—' she held up her index finger – 'they have a suspect in custody.'

'A lead?' Ventnor smiled. 'A breakthrough?'

'Seems so, that's one in Darlington and now one in Sheffield.'

'How many? Oh . . .' Ventnor held up his hand in a gesture of respect for silence. 'Yes, still here. Yes, Philip Bagnall and 541 Finance Company. Really? Well, thank you'. He too replaced his phone. 'That was North Atlantic Utilities, and far from being a salesman who gave up his job with them, he was a salesman who was dismissed by them. He was cold calling and forged a householder's signature. I'll phone Somerled and Reginald back, they'll be interested to know that but he wasn't prosecuted and so he escaped a criminal record, and was able to start a company.'

'Quiet resignation number?'

'Yes . . . pearl-handled revolver or the firing squad . . . so he jumped before he was pushed, but he's a bad lot. So tell me about Sheffield, what's going down there?' Ventnor rose from his chair and walked to the corner of the room to the small table on which stood an electric kettle and a collection of mugs, a tin of tea bags and a jar of coffee. 'Tea?'

'I'm alright, thank you—' Carmen Pharoah patted her stomach – 'I feel awash with the liquid.'

'OK.' Ventnor tested the kettle for weight to determine the amount of water it contained and found it not in need of replenishing from the tap in the kitchen. He switched it on and dropped a tea bag into his mug. He looked up and glanced out of the window, across the car park to the river and the roof line beyond, a contrasting mixture of buildings, ancient and modern.

'Well—' Carmen Pharoah stretched her arms – 'same pattern . . . widowed lady, living in the prestigious suburb of Dore . . .'

Ventnor turned, 'Dore? Yes, I know Dore, prestigious as you say.'

'Well, this lady signed up with 541. They gave her the value of her house and just five years later she was deceased, battered to death in her home. The felon left his prints on the murder weapon, so the conviction was as safe as a house . . . as sound as a pound . . . open and shut case. As in the Hoole case, it was her relatives that questioned the decision to sell her house to 541, very out of character and very shortly after the death of her husband. A Mr and Mrs Lowe, devoted to each other apparently, and it was when she was floating around in a daze of bereavement that she signed away her house. Just the sort of thing a salesman who forges householders' signatures would do.'

'Seems so—' Ventnor poured boiling water into his mug and stirred the tea with his ballpoint pen – 'and the Darlington connection?'

'Carbon copy—' Pharoah glanced at her notebook – 'a not

so elderly person accepted a cheque from 541 and met her maker seven years later. Again, an aggravated burglary, or so it seemed, contents of the house were disturbed but not removed and the police assumed that the burglar had been disturbed or that the intruder had fled in panic once he realized that he had killed the householder. No leads, cold case, lady called Dundas, but the 541 connection is there and once again, it was the relatives who voiced their concerns to the police but no crime was committed in the sense that it's not a crime to buy someone's house, so the police didn't investigate. But the concept of "informed consent" seems to apply in both cases, so they might be able to sue 541 for their inheritance, or Bagnall and Malthouse direct, but that's one for the lawyers.'

'But interesting to find out how much 541 has made.' Ventnor carried his mug of tea back to his desk and sat down.

'We probably will not know the full extent, depends how accurate their records are, how much went unrecorded, but I should think house prices have doubled in the last ten years.'

'Easily—' Ventnor sighed – 'and how many suspect transactions now? I mean which have "matured" in Cobb's words?'

'Twenty-two, and of those, seven matured because of murder, so far as we can tell. We await details of the remaining fifteen but it's still very early days and twenty-two properties, prestigious properties at that, sold within ten years after being purchased, when each house doubled, probably more than doubled in value, that's big money in any man's language and we have one man in Full Sutton for the murder of one such 541 customer. A felon called Rogers, Craig Rogers.'

'Let's go and talk to the boss.' Ventnor stood. 'He'll have to be appraised of this development. Craig Rogers is the breakthrough we've been looking for. The boss will likely want us to pay a call on him.'

Victor Malthouse clearly had the same taste in property as did Philip Bagnall, his house being a similar new build bungalow which occupied a remote field. The one noticeable difference was that Malthouse's bungalow was surrounded by a high, metal fence. Yellich halted the car and Webster got out and pressed the bell at the gate. To his surprise, the gates swung open. He walked through the opening gates and Yellich followed in the car. At the door of the house, they were met by a middle-aged lady in a maid's outfit.

'Police.' Yellich showed her his ID.

'There is but Mr David at home.' The woman spoke with a strongly East European accent.

'He'll do,' Yellich smiled.

'Yes, sir. If you come with me please?' She turned and led the officers into the house, with Yellich and Webster glancing at each other and smiling at the unexpected ease with which they had gained ingress into Victor Malthouse's home. The maid stopped at a door and knocked on it, and entered. 'The police, Mr David.'

'Police!' The voice was nervous, agitated.

'Yes, sir.' The maid stepped aside and Yellich and Webster entered the room.

'David Malthouse?' Yellich asked of the young man in his twenties, casually dressed, as the maid left the vicinity as if returning to her other duties.

'Yes . . .' He seemed pale of face. 'Monika shouldn't have let you in.'

'Well, she did.'

'Dad won't like it; he'll give her the sack. You didn't do her any favours by barging in.'

'We didn't barge in, but, since we are here, perhaps you can help us.'

'What's it about?'

'The 541 Company.'

'Yes . . . that's Dad's company. What about it?'

'We are making inquires . . .'

'Inq—' David Malthouse stammered. 'Ruth phoned earlier, desperate to speak to Dad.'

'Yes, we met her earlier,' Webster explained, 'dare say she wanted to tell your father about us, and that's why Monika knew who we were.'

'Do you work for your father and Mr Bagnall?'

'Yes . . . no . . . sometimes . . . odd jobs. I'm going to university, well that's the plan. What do I tell him?'

'That the police called.'

'About what?'

'The 541 Company . . . and murder.'

'Murder!' David Malthouse swayed unsteadily.

'That's what we want to talk to your father about . . . him and Mr Bagnall, both,' Webster said, and then he added, 'be careful what you get mixed up in, David. You don't seem a bad lad. If you get your paws dirty, you can forget university.'

David Malthouse rocked from side to side, colour drained from his already very pale face.

'Just tell your father we called, and why.' Yellich half turned. 'We'll see ourselves out.'

'Nice meeting you,' Webster added, with a smile.

Driving away from the house, Yellich commented, 'Well, that's the cat set among the pigeons, well and truly so.'

'Oh, I think so.' Webster's eye was caught by a Marsh Harrier swooping low over the meadow. 'What the boss wants, the boss gets.'

Craig Rogers was twenty-seven years old, that by his date of birth. By his hardened attitude and polished survival skills, Carmen Pharoah thought him to be about sixty years, by his psyche, she thought him to be about twelve. He sat in the agent's room of Full Sutton Prison wearing a blue-striped white shirt and denims and sports shoes. He had a deeply pockmarked face, an old scar on his right cheek, and wore his ginger hair closely shaved. He eyed Pharoah and Ventnor with cold suspicion. He drew on the cigarette greedily, holding it delicately between thick, stubby fingers, the nails of which had been bitten to the quick. 'Don't get many visitors.' He inhaled deeply. 'My brother is in the marines, he's a lot younger than me. He's overseas right now. My mum is bad with her nerves, she doesn't leave home except to go shopping . . . mean, one son in the pokey and the other where the bullets are flying, what mother wouldn't be nervy? My brother visits when he's home, he'll keep in touch.'

'How are the days going on?' Ventnor asked.

Rogers shrugged. 'One day at a time. They seem to be leaving me here, no plans for a transfer, so the days sort of . . .'

'Blur?' Pharoah suggested.

'Yes, that's the word, blur, they blur into each other but I'm not a security risk, yet they keep me in Full Sutton.'

'Twenty years,' Pharoah said.

'Minimum.' Craig Rogers breathed deeply. 'Life with a minimum tariff of twenty years, nearly fifty by the time I get out, at least and nothing to come out to, no job, home, family. Can't see a future for myself on the outside. I'm working towards an early parole but for what? After twenty years I might not want to be released. There's old lags in here who fear being released and plan to do something to get banged up again and are doing what they can to avoid parole.'

'You don't come from Sheffield?'

'No, Bradford.'

'So why go to Sheff to burgle?'

Rogers shrugged and drew deeply on the nail. 'Just did, that's all.'

'I know felons don't like to soil their own nests—' Ventnor rested his elbow on the table that stood between him and Rogers – 'and we know that, with the exception of "domestics", husband slays wife or vice versa, we know that the more serious the offence, the further it is committed from the felon's dwelling. So alright, if you burgle, you'll go to the posh end of the city or over to Leeds, to Harrogate or Knaresborough – some big houses there – but not as far south as Sheff. There's a story there.'

'There's a very significant story there.' Pharoah, sitting beside Ventnor also leaned forward. 'Why did you choose that house in Sheffield? And the answer isn't a shrug of your shoulders.'

'That house was targeted for you,' Ventnor pressed, 'by someone who doesn't want to be linked to the murder and

you didn't go there to burgle, you went there to murder the
elderly lady who lived in the house, then . . . then . . .
then . . . you made it look like a burglary. You made it look
like she disturbed you in the middle of rifling through her
things.'

Silence. Rogers drew on the nail, then dogged it in the
Bakelite ashtray. He glanced up at the thick, opaque pane
of glass set in the wall near the ceiling.

'Have you appealed against your sentence?' Pharoah
asked, determined to break the silence.

Rogers shook his head. 'No point.'

'Or were you told not to appeal?'

Rogers glared at Pharoah but remained silent.

'When you were arrested,' she continued, 'you hadn't got
a car or any other form of motor vehicle, no driving licence
either. Mind you that means nothing, people without licences
still drive cars, but the point is that someone drove you to
that house. Somebody pointed that house out to you and you
did the biz but panicked and left the murder weapon with
your prints all over it and a few specs of the victim's blood
on your clothing. So you plead guilty . . . that was sensible . . .
but got life and a high tariff. What did the judge say, "a
premeditated murder of a defenceless, elderly lady, in the
home of, robbing her of a few pence", hence the twenty years.'

'Someone is making this worth your while, isn't that the
case?' Ventnor spoke slowly.

Again, silence.

'How much is twenty years of your life, and arguably
the best twenty? Your young adulthood, how much is that
worth? So, there must be quite a pot of gold out there
waiting for you. I mean, it would take the Gross National
Product of a medium-sized country to make me give up
more than half of my twenties and all my thirties and a bit
of my forties.'

Still a silence.

Outside the door a bunch of keys were jangled noisily.
A door opened and banged shut.

'But you see, Craig—' Carmen Pharoah leaned back in
her chair – 'you don't mind if I call you Craig?'

Rogers shook his head.

'You see, that isn't guaranteed. Whatever has been promised to you, by whomever, is just not guaranteed. Even if the money is lodged somewhere in a high interest account it will be deemed "proceeds of crime" and can be seized.'

Rogers glanced at her. He looked worried.

'That's right, Craig,' Ventnor added, 'especially since we know all about 541.'

'541?'

'541 Finance Co.'

'It means nothing to me that name.'

'OK, so how about the name Bagnall and the name Malthouse,' Ventnor suggested. 'Of the two, we think you'll know Victor Malthouse, he's a blagger, got form for violence and has done time.'

Craig Rogers' eyes narrowed. Those names clearly meant something to him.

'That has reached you, hasn't it?' Carmen Pharoah smiled. 'Your wedge isn't going to be out there when you get out because we are going to lift Bagnall and Malthouse and if they are sensible, they'll start to squeal like a pair of stuck pigs, tell us about you, how much they paid you, that way they work for themselves. We are building a strong case.'

'On the other hand, you could talk to us before they do, give us good information, help us secure a conviction and you could appeal against the twenty-year tariff. Make it worthwhile working towards an early parole and a move to a Category B or even a Category C prison.'

Still a silence.

'We did some checking,' Ventnor said, 'that house in Sheffield was bought by 541 seven years before you murdered the householder.'

'They bought it?'

'Yes . . . didn't you know what they were doing?'

Rogers shook his head.

'Buy a home for peanuts, agree to let the previous owner live there for the rest of their lives but hasten the end of said previous owner's life once the property has substantially increased in value, as in the case of the property you burgled. It had increased by £750,000 in the seven years, a boom time in the property market you see.'

'So 541 made three-quarters of a million pounds in that property, three-quarters of a million pounds following you battering that lady over the head with an iron bar.'

'It's called equity release,' Ventnor explained. 'Lots of legitimate finance companies and insurance companies do it, but they have reserves of millions of pounds and can afford to play by the book and wait for the person to succumb to natural causes, but 541 haven't got those sorts of reserves and seems to want to hurry things along.'

'Which is what you did for them, killing that lady put £75K into their pockets.'

'£75K.' Rogers sighed. 'I'll need to think. I'm not a grass.'

'Well, time presses, Craig, we are looking at a minimum of four other murders. The first person to help us, then we'll help them. If you haven't talked before then, then you'll do your twenty.' Pharoah stood and tapped on the door.

'And still come out to nothing,' Ventnor added, also rising.

Hennessey looked at Shored-Up, who sat in smart clothes. He thought the man looked forlorn, as though he had just woken from a most pleasant dream to find out life was much less attractive. He said so.

'Well, forlorn is the word, Mr Hennessey. I don't know which prison I will be going to. They won't send me to Frankland, that's an assessment prison, they know me too well. So it's Victorian Armley or Full Sutton. Full Sutton is modern but such heavy boys in there. I could hope for the "grey house" in the south, I am over fifty years of age. That would be pleasant, or an open prison, my years and the non-violent nature of my offence. There is a little light at the end of the tunnel, but a good word from your good self at a parole hearing, Mr Hennessey.'

'What happened?' Hennessey glanced round the bare walls of the cell under York Magistrates Court.

'It's a long story but the youth that had the Rolls-Royce keys copied . . .'

'Yes?'

'I should have done it myself. If you want something done, do it yourself. Anyway, he was lifted for a minor offence but he was living under a suspended sentence of two years.'

'Oh?'

'So he was looking at two years in the Young Offenders Institution just for getting disorderly after a few lagers, silly lad. So he wriggled out of it by persuading the police to drop the charges against him in return for information about the theft of a motor vehicle worth tens of thousands of pounds, a good deal for the police. They didn't charge him. He offered them that before he got to the charge bar so they let him sleep it off in the cells and let him go with a warning. Me they huckled at seven o'clock this morning, up before the beaks at ten. Remitted the case to the Crown Court, too heavy for them to handle and refused bail. My sentence will be backdated to today but the premeditation, the value of the car . . . I got a Legal Aid brief who told me that even with a guilty plea, with my track, I could be collecting three or four years, but I will clean the toilets and join the Christian Union and the early parole will be mine.'

'Which is why you asked to see me?'

'Yes . . . you scratch my back . . . one good turn . . .'

'So, what do you have for me?'

'Dunn.'

'Done? Dunn?'

Shored-Up spelled the name. 'Dunn,' he repeated, "Ginger" Dunn.'

'"Ginger" Dunn.' Hennessey took out his notebook and his pen.

'And Clapham Sid.'

'Clapham Sid? Felons?'

'Most felonious of all felons, Mr Hennessey. They were in the den last night, talking about rolling a guy earlier this week. Only meant to hurt him bad but it went further than they intended. Talking freely because the den is full of villains, even the landlord is a blagger. It's a pub load of blaggers.'

'Be good of you to tell me what its real name is.'

'Can't even do that Mr Hennessey, so it's just "the den", but the information is kosher. Flashing his money about, got well paid for the job but Clapham Sid, he's the boy, the lad of the duo, he's scared, he's your mark, he'll fold before "Ginger" Dunn.'

'Where can we find them?'

'Don't know, but they both have form, it won't be hard. But you'll put a word in for me at my parole hearing? I really need a good word because Miss Pratt told me that if I ever got arrested she will only be able to report that I had . . . what was the word she used? Indifferent, that was it. I had an indifferent attitude to my probation order, attending interviews as if under duress.'

'Well you were, Shored-Up, you were.' Hennessey stood. 'But, yes, if this checks out—' he patted his notepad – 'if this gets us a result, then yes, a good word from me at the eventual parole hearing is guaranteed.'

'Didn't take you long to think,' Carmen Pharoah said with a smile as she and Ventnor walked back into the agents' room at HM Prison, Full Sutton.

Craig Rogers looked down at the table top. 'Glad they were able to stop you before you left the prison, saved you a drive back, but I got twenty years and they pocket three quarters of a million . . . three quarters of a million!'

'So, what happened?' Ventnor sat beside Carmen Pharoah in the chairs they had vacated just a few moments earlier.

'It was Victor Malthouse. He gave me fifty thousand pounds, drove me to the house, told me what to do, make sure the old girl was iced and then make it look like a burglary gone pear-shaped. He drove me there and drove me back to Bradford. We did time together once, that's how we know each other. He gave me fifty and he and Bagnall got seven hundred and fifty. You're right, they cheated me, it's not the fifty for twenty years, it's that they cheated me.'

'Even so, fifty thousand pounds for twenty years – selling yourself cheap there, Craig.'

'Well, what do they say? One man's floor is another

man's ceiling. I was living rough, Salvation Army shelters. I was doing nothing, going nowhere, so a cot and three for twenty years and a wedge to come out to seemed a good idea at the time.'

'Where's the money now?'

'Spent it.' Rogers smiled. 'All gone.'

Ventnor returned the smile. 'You mean Malthouse paid you fifty thousand pounds in cash so we can't trace it and you put the £50K into a high yield building society account which is giving ten per cent compound per annum and you posted the passbook to your brother in the Royal Marines for safe keeping?'

Rogers shrugged and smiled again. 'So, do you want a statement, and an agreement to turn Queen's evidence in open court, or don't you?'

It was Friday, 16.50 hours.

Saturday, 09.50 hours.

'There is,' said Hennessey, 'a pleasant sense of achievement in closing down on two felons without ever having met either, which is sometimes the case in police work. I find it neater somehow, just planting a whole pile of evidence in front of someone and saying, "Right, get out of that". Hennessey paused. 'All they can do in that situation is go "G", as my son would say, to go "NG" would be suicidal.'

'Indeed.' Yellich nodded as he followed Hennessey along the cell corridor in the basement of Michlegate Bar Police Station. 'I do so dislike seeing felons walk out of custody because there just is not enough to hold them, even when we all know they are guilty.'

'To see Sydney Liddle—' Hennessey approached the custody sergeant's desk – 'DCI. Hennessey and DS Yellich, of this police station.'

'Yes, sir.' The custody sergeant wrote the officers' names in the ledger and noted the time of their arrival in the custody suite. 'We put him in interview room one, sir, as you requested.'

'Interview room one, thank you. How is he?'

'Indignant.' The custody sergeant smiled. 'They all make

their presence known by one means or another and young
Sydney is very indignant. "He hate da north of England."
'The custody sergeant imitated a south London accent
pronouncing 'hate' as 'ate' and 'north' as 'nawf'. '"I want
to go to Wandsworth. Why can't I go to Wandsworth" and
pronouncing "Wandsworth" as "Wonds-wuff", so I told him
he should have stayed in the smoke to do his crooking, silly
lad.'

'That's useful to know,' said Hennessey smiling.
'Something we can offer him in return for cooperation.
Interview room one, you say?'

Sydney 'Clapham Sid' Liddle was, Hennessey and Yellich
saw, a slightly built youth with penetrating, angry-looking
eyes, and was heavily bruised about the face. He seemed
to have a vicious edge to him, the sort of boy who'd be a
low-order member of a street gang, the one who would
wade in with pointed toed shoes once the victim was on
the deck. He was about five feet tall and underweight.
Hennessey thought that were he an animal, he'd be a weasel.

'Gather you know "Ginger" Dunn.' Hennessey sat opposite
Liddle. Yellich sat next to Hennessey.

Sydney Liddle's eyes narrowed.

'So you do know him?'

'Saying nothing,' pronouncing nothing as 'naffin', exactly
as the custody sergeant had imitated.

'Southern boy,' Hennessey observed, 'by your accent.'

'Yeah.' Liddle looked at the floor and replied sulkily.

'London?'

'Yeah.'

'Clapham? I mean, your nickname . . .'

'Yeah.'

'Don't know Clapham. I'm from Greenwich. Same side
of the river, a bit further east.'

'Yeah.' But this time there was enthusiasm in Liddle's
voice and a smile as he looked up at Hennessey. 'London
pride, eh,' he said.

'Yes, as you say, Sydney, London pride. Dare say you
want to go home?'

'Too right . . . the north isn't for me.'

'So why are you here?'

'Stupidity—' Liddle rolled his eyes – 'plain stupidity.'

'Well—' Hennessey relaxed his body language – 'ninety per cent of the prison population are where they are because of some form of stupidity.'

'The other ten per cent?'

'Wrongful convictions, insanity, that sort of thing.'

'You mean you do get it wrong?' Liddle smiled a thin smile.

'So who's perfect? So tell me about your act of stupidity.'

'Well, I kept myself alive by ducking and diving and bobbing and weaving, you know the game. I just done detention centres before, reckon I'm for the big home now,' he added with a smile. 'That's where I need to be.'

'Yes, we're after you for the murder of Edwin Hoole a few days ago. We just need his blood on your clothes . . . and you made a right mess of him.'

'I didn't, Dunn did, he's mad.' Liddle pointed to his face. 'He did this to me.'

'So, you're admitting it?' Hennessey smiled. 'Saves us all a lot of trouble.'

'My dad, he always said, if the Old Bill have you bang to rights, just start working for yourself. So, yeah, you'll find the old boy's blood on my clothes, my shoes . . . I watch television . . . even the smallest bit you can't see with your eye, just that little bit is enough to put you away.'

'Yes, that's true,' Yellich advised.

'Dunn's flown, soon as we lifted you he flew. He must have been tipped off. So he's guilty, only the guilty run, but we'll pick him up, he can't stay submerged for ever, and he'll likely blame you.'

'Me? My size?' Liddle smiled and shook his head. 'He can try. But Dunn did the damage, it was all done by Dunn. Dunn done it. I kept saying to him we were only supposed to warn him but Dunn, he just didn't stop battering him with a length of lead piping. He had that crazy look in his eyes.'

'To warn him of what?'

'To stop asking questions.'

'Who paid you?'

'Fella called Bagnall. Well, he paid Dunn really and Dunn gave me a wedge. Dunn works for Bagnall and Bagnall's friend, fella called Malthouse. He's worked for them for a few years. Him and me, once or twice, but mainly him.'

'Really?'

'Yeah? Can I get a transfer to Wandsworth? I got mates in Wandsworth.'

'Yes—' Hennessey sat forward – 'you can request a transfer if you're doing more than an eight stretch, and if we tell the prison service that you cooperated.'

'An eight stretch,' he said, looking pleased and proud.

'You're looking at life, conspiracy to murder, not the full life tariff though, you'll get out soon enough. So, what did Dunn do with the murder weapon?'

'Stored it in the shed in his garden. He's used it a few times. He told me he used it on a woman in her house, then carried her old body out to some nearby woods and left her there. Dare say her blood will be on it as well. He's fond of it. You see, that's Dunn, he's mad. Any other villain would have launched it into the river but Dunn likes it, so he keeps it. It'll convict him.'

'So how did you know where Mr Hoole would be?'

'We followed him, waiting for a time to do the business. Then he drove his Jaguar out of town and met a guy, leaving his Jag parked up in a remote place, drove off in the other guy's car. So "Ginger" Dunn, he says we'll wait, he'll get dropped back there to pick his car up by the other geezer and if the other geezer doesn't hang around then that's where and when we'll earn the money.'

'Which is what happened?'

'Yes, that's how it went down. We left Dunn's van on the road so we wouldn't leave no tyre tracks. We waited in the shadows, rained all the time, then the geezer was brought back, the other guy just drove off, didn't wait to see him safely in his car. So we pounced and did the business. All over very quickly really. On the way back Dunn kept going on about a red mist that comes over him when he does violence. So, be careful when you lift him, he won't come quietly.'

'Thanks for the warning. You're on your way to Wandsworth.'

'I am?' Liddle's eyes brightened. 'The big "M" too, reckon I'm a player now, reckon there will be an opening for me in the villainy in London. The big "M" opens doors.'

'So what does Dunn do for Bagnall and Malthouse?'

'Ices folk. He's their hit man.'

'Always batters?'

'Not always. He told me that once Bagnall and Malthouse wanted a murder to look like natural causes, if that was possible, so Dunn, he used a plastic bag on an old geezer and switched the television on, and other than that, touched nothing, but he was careful to take the bag away with him. Other times he used his van or some other car . . . ran people down or forced them off the road.'

'Good, so all we need now is a statement.'

Liddle laughed. 'You're not getting that. No, this is off the record. I won't get nowhere if I grass anybody up. No, I've told you where to find the murder weapon. I told you how it went down. I've told you that Dunn is a hit man and I'll also tell you that if you search Dunn's drum you'll likely find trophies from his victims' homes.'

'You're working against yourself now,' Hennessey growled, 'we'd have found the murder weapon anyway and the proceeds of burglary.'

Liddle shook his head. 'No, I'm working for myself, doing my bird and not grassing in exchange for an early release, that will give me street cred and you wouldn't have found the murder weapon. It's not so much in the shed at the bottom of his garden as under it, like buried and wrapped in canvas. You wouldn't have found it but now you can say you found it because you made a good search. Helps you and keeps me right, and the trophies, you wouldn't see them as proceeds of burglary because they have no value but the relatives of his victims would recognize their dad's old cigarette lighter or their mum's hatpin and one such by itself might not mean anything but they're all in a fruit bowl on top of his hi-fi system.' Liddle sat back and grinned. 'You see, you'd have missed those, you wouldn't have seen their significance would you? Dunn's done a few contracts for Bagnall and Malthouse and when he could, he helped himself to a little trophy of no value at all. Only he knows what they represented.'

'And now we do,' Yellich added, conceding that Liddle had a point.

'Yes, but that's all on the q. t. Now I expect you to work for me on the q. t. Now you have evidence for a safe conviction for a series of murders. So you owe me. I'll plead guilty to one conspiracy to murder and other than that it's "no comment".'

Philip Bagnall came quietly, meekly in fact, thought the officer who arrested him at his home in front of his shocked wife. He climbed quietly into the rear of the police car and said not a word during the drive to Micklegate Bar Police Station where he was cautioned and placed in an interview room. When George Hennessey and Somerled Yellich entered the room he spoke for the first time. 'I am pleased it's all over,' he said smiling. 'It's like a weight falling from my shoulders.'

Hennessey saw a round-faced man, casually but well dressed and who had a gentle manner and could perhaps be described as appearing, but only appearing, to be kindly.

'Good,' Hennessey replied softly. 'I am pleased for you, Mr Bagnall.'

'Call me Philip.'

'Philip.' It was, thought Hennessey, a strange and misplaced attempt at friendship but he was content to oblige. 'Good for you.'

'I just do stupid things. If people suggest them, I do them. I suppose you could say that I am easily led. It gets the better of my thinking, especially if there's a bit of pressure. I shouldn't have been self-employed. I don't do well under pressure. I would have been better employed, let someone else have the stress. You know I once lost my job as a salesman for forging a customer's signature . . .'

'We know, we checked up on you before arresting you.'

'I didn't think they'd tell you that.'

'Well, they did. We told them it was a murder inquiry.'

'That's what I do. I would never have dreamed of doing that until another member of the sales team suggested I do it. I hadn't made a sale for weeks and it was a commission-only post, so no sale meant no money. So, one rainy day, in winter, knocking on doors, one door was opened by this weedy looking, absent-minded guy and I thought, "I'll risk it".' Bagnall shook his head. 'Turned out he was a barrister specializing in criminal law. He complained in writing so the company had his real signature against my forgery, so I got the chop.'

'Then what?'

'Then I met Victor Malthouse and Ruth de Vries. They had some money and I had a little inheritance. Used it to buy a Bentley and the rest went to 541, set it up with Victor and Ruth. Returns were slow. We were lending out but it was slow coming back in. The equity release was particularly slow. Huge companies, the high street names, they can wait as long as they have to but we couldn't, we needed a quicker return.'

'You have been cautioned,' Hennessey reminded him.

'Yes, and offered a lawyer—' he glanced at the glowing red light and the twin cassettes of the tape recorder spinning slowly – 'and I realize this interview is being taped . . . in accordance with an Act of Parliament.'

'Police and Criminal Evidence Act 1985,' Hennessey advised him, 'known as "PACE".'

'OK.'

'So . . . by speed up, what do you mean?'

'Help folks on their way to the hereafter or the not so far off, as my grandmother used to call it.'

'Details, please. Specifically you mean what?'

'Murder.' Bagnall spoke flatly, matter-of-factly.

'Thank you.' Hennessey wondered if Bagnall was being reached by the enormity of the situation he was in but he repeated, 'Thank you.'

'Whom did you hire?'

'Malthouse took care of that side of things. Is he here? Have you arrested him as well?'

'No, he's done a runner but he won't get far.'

'Oh.' Again a strange absence of interest.

'So what happened?'

'Well, the problem was that Malthouse targeted folk who had a lot of life in them and quite naturally people began to get suspicious. Then that fella started asking questions. He phoned us up and identified himself, told us what he was going to do, so we knew who he was. Malthouse hired two thugs to talk him out of it but they murdered him, that wasn't the plan, not the plan at all.'

'Sadly so.'

'This is Ruth's doing. She wanted to wring the Hoole family dry. She felt she was cheated in the divorce settlement even though she did well out of it. So me, the salesman with the gift of the smooth talk called on her former brother-in-law when he was at a low ebb after the loss of his wife and he signed the forms and accepted a cheque.'

'Did you have anything to do with his wife being killed? She was run down. We believe she could have been mistaken for her husband. They were walking home. She was dressed in a similar manner and unusually, she was on the outside.'

Bagnall looked to his left with widening eyes. 'I can see that, that never occurred to me but I can see Ruth wanting that done, even getting behind the wheel of her car and doing it herself. She was just burning up with hatred for the Hoole family and looked very pleased when Harold Hoole was found dead. A stroke they said it was, which is what Victor hoped for.'

'So Malthouse arranged that?'

'He arranged all of them. There was the last boom in house prices, a lot of properties we bought tripled in value in ten years, less sometimes. But the maturing of the policy on Harold Hoole's house really seemed to please Ruth. It was as if Victor had done it to please her. Is she arrested?'

'Nope—' Hennessey shook his head – 'but we'll find her. She's likely with Malthouse. Two fugitives together are twice as easy to find. So how many murders are we talking about?'

'Dunno—' Bagnall opened the palms of his hands – 'but

we didn't make as much as it looks like on paper because the hit men had to be paid, but possibly seven or eight policies were matured ahead of their time. We cleared seven figures comfortably so. Reckon we will lose that now, proceeds of crime . . .'

'Reckon you will.'

'So, life for me. Suppose I had better get used to being on the inside.'

'Well, a guilty plea, full cooperation with the remainder of this investigation – you'll breathe free air again at some point.'

'But not for a likely time.'

'No—' Hennessey shook his head briefly – 'not for a likely time. So, let's get all this down in the form of a statement. This is where you start to work for yourself.'

It was Saturday, 11.47 hours.

EPILOGUE

The man and the woman walked barefoot on the sand in the moonlight, to their left the lights of the hotels, to their right the inky black waters of the Adriatic.

'We never did get to the bottom of it but that's often the way of it. Some more of their customers were likely murdered by them, we just couldn't prove it.'

'Even with Bagnall's confession?'

'Malthouse discredited him as much as he could, said that Bagnall was over-egging his statement to serve his own ends and we couldn't identify all the hit men they used, really just Sydney "Clapham Sid" Liddle and "Ginger" Dunn and those two did the best out of it really.'

'Oh?' The woman glanced at the man.

'Well, Liddle got his conviction for conspiracy to murder so he's doing his rite of passage number. He'll get his transfer to Wormwood Scrubs or Wandsworth where he can make contact with the London crews, be set for a life of crime when he does come out and Dunn was found to be NG by reason of insanity and will spend the rest of his life in a secure hospital. The other three, Bagnall, Malthouse and de Vries all started to condemn each other in the dock and collected seven life sentences to run concurrently, as you will have read.'

'And proceeds seized?'

'Yes, but they are contesting the legality of that so the proceeds haven't been seized so much as frozen, so that will rumble on in the civil courts for a while.'

'And the other customers who lived?'

'Ah . . . that is the good news, we advised them of the legal notion of "informed consent" and last we heard they were raising legal action to have the contracts declared null and void, and since 541 has ceased all trading anyway, it looks like they'll get their houses back and get to keep the money they sold them for.'

'Neat—' the woman squeezed the man's arm – 'very neat. I like that outcome.'

There was a splash to their right.

'What was that?' asked George Hennessey.

'Dolphin,' replied Louise D'Acre. 'Probably a dolphin, they come close in shore at night.'